THE RAGGED MAN'S COMPLAINT

James Robertson was born in 1958 and grew up in Bridge of Allan, Stirlingshire. He studied history at Edinburgh University, later returning to complete a doctorate on the works of Sir Walter Scott. Other occupations have brought him in contact with frozen food, lions, monkeys, ice, fruit trees, building sites, gold, mud, wholefoods and books. His first collection of short stories *Close* was published in 1991. He is the first holder of the Brownsbank Writing Fellowship based at the former home of Hugh MacDiarmid near Biggar.

D1434758

THE RAGGED MAN'S COMPLAINT

JAMES ROBERTSON

And, thus as we wer talking to and fro,
We saw a boustious berne cum ouir the bent,
But hors, on fute, als fast as he mycht go,
Quhose rayment was all raggit, revin and rent,
With visage leyne, as he had fastit lent:
And fordwart fast his wayis he did advance,
With ane rycht malancolious countynance.

Sir David Lindsay, "The Complaynt of the Commoun Weill of Scotland",
from *The Dreme of Schir David Lyndesay* (1528).

EDINBURGH
B&W PUBLISHING
1993

First published 1993
by B&W Publishing
Edinburgh
Copyright © James Robertson
ISBN 1 873631 24 3

The publisher acknowledges subsidy
from the Scottish Arts Council towards
the publication of this volume.

British Library Cataloguing in Publication Data:
A catalogue record for this book is available from
the British Library

Cover photograph and design by Harry Palmer

Printed by Werner Söderström

THE RAGGED MAN'S COMPLAINT

1	Giraffe	1
2	The Plagues	17
3	Screen Lives	25
4	The Jonah	33
5	The Claw	46
6	Squibs	54
7	Bastards	62
8	Facing It	71
9	The End Is Nigh	72
10	The Mountain	77
11	What Love Is	95
12	Portugal 5, Scotland 0	105
13	Tilt	107
14	Surprise Surprise	127
15	Republic of the Mind	133
16	Pretending To Sleep	150

Acknowledgements

I owe my thanks to Biggar Museum Trust for creating the Brownsbank Writing Fellowship and appointing me as its first recipient. Without their support, and the generous sponsorship of the Fellowship by Strathclyde Regional Council, Clydesdale District Council and the Scottish Postal Board, the completion of this book would have been a much longer and more daunting task.

Lines from Hugh MacDiarmid's poem "The Innumerable Christ" appear with the kind permission of Michael Grieve.

Raymond Carver's essay "On Writing" appears in *Fires: Essays, Poems, Stories*.

for my parents

Giraffe

The day Eilidh died. It started with a hangover and got worse. That's how Jimmy Sanderson minds it.

He minds doing the meat-run that day, feeling like shite, him and Eck down at the mink farm loading up the dead beasts. "There's a wee treat for the cats in the horse-box," Murray had said, but he hadn't said what. Jimmy can still picture himself, clear as anything, flicking up the snecks to let down the back of the box. It was full of horses' heads—twenty or thirty of them—and pathetic wee bundles of dead lambs in plastic bags.

"Fuck's sake," said Eck.

It was May, and very hot. The heads had been lying for days and some of the eyes were out on their stalks. Up until that moment Jimmy'd always thought that only happened in cartoons.

Still feeling rough with the drink he grabbed a couple of heads by the lugs and swung them up into the meat-trailer where they landed with a thud. "Right," he said. "May as well get this ower wi."

After a few seconds Eck stamped out his fag and joined him. "Need tae pit these out o sight," he said. "Where the punters canna see them."

First there was the hangover, then getting a roasting from Murray for being late in, then the meat-run with those heads from the knackers, then Eilidh dying. And the dead monkey, don't forget the dead monkey. That was a lot of bad things for one day, even for the Park.

Jimmy had been out on the bevvy with Eck the night before and he'd stayed over at Eck's because he couldn't ride his bike home in the state he was in. Eck's ma was supposed to wake them at half-seven but she must have been drunker than both of

1

them because she never did, the first thing Jimmy knew about the morning was the sun hitting him in the eyes through a gap in the living-room curtains and himself swimming off the couch with a full bladder and a burst skull. Eck's ma was still snoring when they left the house ten minutes after they should have been at work. Jimmy got the bike started (at least he'd had the sense to leave it at Eck's before they hit the pubs) and Eck jumped on behind and somehow Jimmy managed to get them to the Park without putting the bike in the sheuch, the bevvy sloshing around in his head every time they leaned into a curve.

They were only half an hour late but Murray gave them a bollocking just the same. "This isna a fuckin holiday camp by the way." Jimmy was going to say, "Well, it is, kinna," but thought better of it. "I'm dockin an hour aff your wages, the pair o yous," said Murray. "You're lucky you're no gettin your buiks." He'd already sent Dave Maxton to let out the giraffes and camels. That would be all that he'd done, you could bet on it. Maxton was one lazy bad bastard. Jimmy and Eck got given the meat-run which didn't exactly help the queasy feeling in Jimmy's belly. A couple of sheep for the tigers, an old cow and some heads for the female lions, some more heads and the lambs for the males. Eck had gutted the big beasts the day before, but Murray had forgotten to tell him about the stuff in the horse-box till that morning. Jimmy said, "Are we gaunae huv tae gut the lambs an aa?" but Eck shook his head. "They can hae the fuckin lot." In the lion sections they dropped the heads behind fallen tree-trunks so as not to upset the public when they drove by.

They were back at the office an hour later, waiting on orders, which was when Murray exploded off the phone about the monkey. The second one in a week. Apparently it was lying on the hard shoulder of the motorway, about four miles across country from the Park. "That's quite a hike for a wee Injun bandit in hostile fermin territory," Eck commented. (He was a great man for the Westerns.) Some concerned motorist had phoned in to complain. Murray was not a happy man.

"How dae the fuckers get out, that's whit I want tae ken.

2

We've been roun that perimeter fence three fuckin times. An how come they ayeweys end up on the fuckin roads? I mean, could they no juist disappear intae the hills or somethin, for fuck's sake?"

It was embarrassing. For the Park, that is. Personally, it didn't put Jimmy up nor down. He wasn't even that bothered about the thing getting squashed, truth was he wasn't fond of the monkeys and his head was killing him.

"It must be a hole but," said Eck. "There's nae wey these monkeys can get ower the tap, no wi the electric strands an the wey it angles in."

Murray gave him a look. "I don't need you tae tell me that," he said. That wasn't what was bothering him, it was the bad publicity.

"I'm juist sayin," said Eck.

"Ay, aa right," said Murray. "Away and check the bluidy fence again. Jimmy, you go doun an kick Dave Maxton's airse. I better go an pick the bugger up afore the Salvation Army get on the phone."

As Murray drove away, the first cars of the day were just going through the lock-gates into the tiger section. Jimmy headed off to the giraffe-house to see what Maxton hadn't got up to, and to have a look at Eilidh.

Rhesus monkeys. The Park only had them because they were easier to manage than the baboons. The baboons were before Jimmy's time, and they'd had to go. They were maladjusted. They systematically ripped people's cars to pieces. They weren't intimidated by human beings or human devices at all. Somebody had to stand at the section exit with a long bamboo pole and knock them off from under the cars to stop them escaping. After closing-time they went over the fence anyway—using the shock from the electrified strands to give them an extra boost—and roamed through the woods at the back of the Park jumping out at evening joggers and strollers. Drunk men arrived home to their wives with tales of hairy old satanists scampering naked through the undergrowth. The baboons came back to the Park before dawn so that they wouldn't miss out on any food that was going. The final straw was when half the troop turned up at a funeral in the nearest village. Uninvited. Whenever Jimmy thought of that it was the uninvited bit that made him laugh. He could see the baboons sitting po-faced and blue-arsed on the gravestones, wearing tall black hats and stroking their chins, being cold-shouldered by the other mourners. The local paper made a fuss and they had to go, back to Africa or Longleat or wherever they'd come from.

But then, as Eck said, nobody could be sure they'd caught them all. Baboons weren't daft—some of them might have opted to stay out. They might be out there yet.

It was a rat that killed Eilidh, Jimmy's pretty sure of it. Not in the long term of course. He has a theory about that too, about captivity and exploitation and living conditions. But in the short term, as an immediate cause of death, he'd put his money on a rat.

She didn't mind about the rats if she had company. She could deal with them if the other giraffes were in the stall with her. But in the period before her death she'd been on her own a lot. They'd had to keep her in the yard, or sometimes in the stall, when the others went out each morning. Some days the vet was coming to see her, or she had to be put in the crush to get the wound treated, or she was stumbling around so much she was a danger to herself and to the people having their picnics. Towards the end it was the smell of the wound as much as anything. Murray had enough complaints on his hands what with the squashed monkeys. Some do-gooder was always trying to spot animals in poor condition. So Eilidh was stuck inside all day, stretching her neck out into the sunlight through the top half-doors, on her own, not coping with the rats. She was a sad case.

Nobody knew quite how the wound on her front left leg had started, but probably it was from a sharp point on one of the fences. Jimmy felt a bit guilty because he should have spotted it sooner. Either the metal was rusty or the wound had got septic

4

some other way, but before long it was weeping and expanding in a big oval patch that Eilidh made worse by rubbing it against the trees and fences all day. Murray and Jimmy got her into the crush and cleaned it up and sprayed it with purple disinfectant but it didn't improve. Then she started limping with it. The vet came and told them to treat it daily. It fell to Jimmy to organise this. It would take two or three of them to coax her into the crush, tempting her with food and prodding her in the oxters with the bamboo poles, but after a while she associated the crush with the pain of disinfecting the wound and it became harder to get her in. Food no longer tempted her as she was eating virtually nothing. She became more and more difficult; you couldn't help getting impatient with her. Maxton said the only thing the animals understood was pain, if you hit the bastards hard enough they would do what you wanted. He demonstrated this by giving the male camel a flying kick in the bollocks to prove he could get it into its shed at night when nobody else could. The camel went—spitting and gurgling, but it went. Maxton also tried his theory out on Stumpy, a wee elephant without its tail that had been dumped on the Park from one of the Company's places in England. Maxton regularly battered Stumpy across the head and trunk with an old table-leg, to show who was boss. It worked. Whenever he saw Maxton coming, Stumpy backed into a corner of the yard, watching him warily. "That's great, Dave," said Jimmy. "If the rest o us take turns tae beat him senseless he'll respect us all." "He's fuckin dangerous," Maxton retorted. "Ye've tae fuckin watch him." "Ay, nae fuckin wunner," said Jimmy. One of his fantasies was that Stumpy would grow tusks overnight and staple the bastard to a tree. Around that time he hated having his day off if Maxton was working it, he didn't like to think what he might be doing to Eilidh. It was a relief coming back and finding her still limping and thrawn, still stinking of gangrene.

One morning—this was a week or so before she died—Jimmy was up on the walk in the giraffe-house checking the feed in the troughs. Eilidh didn't hear him coming. Even before he reached the stall he could tell something was wrong. Up there he was on

5

a level with Eilidh's head, but she didn't notice him at all. She was wedged into one corner, her flanks quivering, her big soft eyes fixed in terror on the opposite corner of the stall, where a huge wet rat was scuffling around in the straw. The rat wasn't paying Eilidh a blind bit of notice. One well-aimed kick from her would have splattered it all over the walls. But she couldn't move. Jimmy'd seen her nervous often enough—the giraffes were skeerie, easily spooked—but he'd never seen fear like that in her before. That's how, later, he was certain it was a rat, maybe even the same rat, that finished her off.

There were two stalls, each big enough to take four giraffes at night. One of the things that had to be done every second day was move Eilidh from one stall to the other so they could be mucked out. For several days before she died Jimmy had tried to shift her and failed, she was getting that stubborn. So this morning he arrived at the giraffe-house with his head pounding knowing she would have to be moved. Maxton was propped up on some sacks of feed in the store-room, drinking tea and smoking. "Did ye shift Eilidh?" He might as well have asked if he'd been up Ben Ledi before breakfast, the look Maxton gave him. "Did I fuck. Fuckin bitch willna fuckin shift." Jimmy had a sore head, he wasn't in the mood to take Maxton on. He was trouble, everybody knew that. Of course he hadn't mucked out the empty stall either. Jimmy just went on and did it himself.

It was while he was in there that the crash came in the other stall. A terrible thumping crash followed by a scrabbling, thrashing sound. He tried to jump up onto the walk from the floor but it was too high, so he had to run all the way back across the yard and in through the store-room. Maxton was still lounging around. "Whit's the fuckin hurry?" When Jimmy got to Eilidh's stall it was almost over. She was backed into that same corner, but this time she'd gone down with all her legs tangled up underneath her. When she saw the rat she must have slipped in her panic on the sharn that hadn't been mucked out, and she was too weak to stop herself falling. She was struggling to keep her neck upright against the wall but it was no good, what strength she had was going into the useless flailing of her

6

legs. Jimmy couldn't get near her. For all that she was weakened and timid she still had enough power in those legs to kill him if she connected a kick. He couldn't even reach over to support her head, and all the time he could hear her breathing becoming more desperate. The giraffes were odd like that. They never made a noise, and they could only sit down with a special folding arrangement of the legs. Any other way and they couldn't get up again, and what was more the length of their necks made it impossible for them to breathe properly if they weren't upright. He shouted on Maxton to get Murray on the radio but then he minded he was away for the dead monkey, out of range, so all he could do was hunker down on the walk and watch the life ebb out of Eilidh. That's how he sees it now: sitting watching her, thinking, this is a crime, this is not the way a giraffe should die. But she died anyway. He never even saw the rat, but for days after that if he caught one in the open he would go after it with a spade and batter it to bits.

Maxton appeared on the walk beside him. He took a drag on his cigarette and flicked ash in the direction of Eilidh's corpse. "About fuckin time," he said. "Least we'll no hae tae bother wi thon fuckin crush ony mair." Maxton hadn't helped with the crush for a week at least. Jimmy pushed past him. "Fuck off, Maxton. Juist fuck off, right?" He went out into the fresh air. Behind him he heard Maxton saying, "Away an fuckin greit then."

Jimmy thought only people in *The Sunday Post* were called Eck until he met Eck Galbraith. His ma in a moment of insanity (not the first or last by a long stroke, according to Eck) had named him and his twin brother Hector and Lysander, and they'd had to go through life disguising themselves as Eck and Sandy. Eck had been at the Park longer than Murray and even though Murray was the boss Eck had a way of getting round him. He could give him lip and get away with it when anybody else would have got a smack in the face. It was as if he had something on Murray. He always managed to get the easy work, or at least the work that was most out of the way and least supervised. Like for example he'd persuaded Murray that he knew all about butchering and could therefore be entrusted with preparing the meat for the cats. This was crap—he'd never cut up anything bigger than an ashet pie—but he learned by trial and error before Murray was wise to him, and nobody else got near the meat-room after that. Also he was one of the few workers whose driving licence was still unmarked, so he could be allowed out on the public roads with a tractor and trailer, going round the neighbouring farms to pick up the cheap cows, sheep, horses and other corpses that the Park fed to its beasts. Eck was left pretty much to his own devices, and early on Jimmy had seen it was a good ploy to get in with him and get a share in some of the cushy numbers. Not that he minded working with the giraffes and camels. They were easy, most of the time. But it was good to get away from the crowds once in a while, down the back road to the old mink farm which was where all the fruit, feed, hay and straw was stored. The stink of bananas down there—he couldn't eat a banana for years after he worked at the Park. Next to the stores was the meat-room, where Eck got to practise with his big knives, gutting the beasts and freezing what couldn't be used straightaway. The freezer was something out of a horror picture: whole beasts—mostly sheep—gutted and flung on the heap where they froze with their legs all twisted and sticking out at grotesque angles. Nobody was quite sure if everything in there was hundred per cent safe, so they tended to use fresh meat whenever possible. So long as the vet had given it the nod. No point in introducing foot-and-mouth or something into the Scottish lion population. (This was years ago, of course. Mad-cow disease wasn't even invented in these days.)

Eck knew everything there was to know about working in the Park. When Jimmy first started, Eck filled him in on all the characters. He warned him about Dave Maxton. "That bastart's gaunae end up back in the jyle." Then there was old John, one of the gatekeepers, who'd been three years in a P.O.W. camp in the war, and had never got over it. He used to shout abuse and wave his shotgun around at any carload of Japanese that came through. But they couldn't understand what he was on about, they probably thought he was part of the show. Another old guy, Wull Telfer, used to take the chimp island boat across the artificial river and set snares for rabbits on the edge of the farmland there. Sometimes he'd take one of the Park's guns, load up with his own cartridges, and try for a pheasant or two. A fierce auld bugger was Wull. But when he got home on a Friday he had to hand over his wage-packet unopened or his wife would batter him, and if he wanted a smoke he had to get out of the house and do it in the toolshed.

There was Gav, who when he got married they stripped him naked, sprayed his balls with purple dye and drove him through the tiger section tied to the bonnet of a landrover. There was Annie up at the restaurant, who stood up on a table at a Park disco one night and challenged all the white hunters to arm-wrestling. "White hunters!" she snorted, meaning the guys who drove the zebra-striped landrovers in the cat sections. "Think ye're in the fuckin Serengeti or somethin." Nobody took up the challenge. Once there were two year-old lion cubs that had been taken off their mother to be trained for the circus. They turned on a guy called Andy who'd gone into their cage to play with them, to impress Annie, and Annie went in after him and dragged him out, beating the cubs off with her handbag. This was the same Andy that had an artificial hand because he'd blown the real one off some time before, making a bomb, or so Eck claimed. It was never clear what he wanted the bomb for. "Dinna ken," said Eck. "Maybe he was gaunae blaw up the oil pipeline tae England or somethin. He doesna like fowk talkin about his haun by the way."

Eck and Jimmy were out on the randan and Eck was playing pool with a guy he knew called Iain. Jimmy was chatting to this lassie that was with Iain, he'd seen her around before and quite fancied her. She was impressed by the fact that he worked at the Park.

"It must be brilliant, workin wi the animals an that. I love animals."

"Ay, it's aa right," said Jimmy casually. You didn't want to

9

be too enthusiastic, sound like a wee boy. Anyway it wasn't that great. "The pay's shite," he said. "Thirty-nine pound for a fifty-four hour week. I could maybe get somethin else but I'd miss bein outside."

"Is it no dangerous?" she said. Her name was Carol. She worked in Boots in the new shopping-centre. She had short dark hair and bright red lips and Jimmy bet she'd look great in one of those white chemist's coats.

"Naw, no really," he said, playing it dead casual still. "No unless ye're stupit." He thought of the game he and Gav had been playing the week before. You parked your landrover behind the male lions and let them sit dozing for a while, forgetting you were there. Then when there were no punters about one of you had to run out and boot the nearest lion up the arse and get back to the landrover before it woke up and came after you. Gav did it first. Then Jimmy had to do it. As soon as he kicked the lion he heard Gav starting up the motor and backing away at top speed. Jimmy nearly shat himself catching up with him, then they couldn't stop laughing for half an hour. The funniest thing was the lion never even stirred. They'd have been in more danger from Murray if he'd seen them at it.

"These lions are fucked," said Gav. "There's nae fuckin lion left in them."

Jimmy said, "Did ye ever see that film about the Stones at Altamont? When they hired the Hell's Angels tae act as security an peyed them in beer?"

"That wis responsible," said Gav.

"Ay," said Jimmy. "Well, things are gettin a bit out o haun, an Mick's up on the stage tryin tae cool it, he's gaun, ''Ere, which cats wanna fite?' I tell ye, it wisna these yins onywey."

"These cats wouldna fight wi fuckin dugs," said Gav.

"Ay, it's pretty safe," Jimmy said to Carol, "if ye're no daft." She was looking at him admiringly. He glanced over at Iain and Eck at the pool-table. Iain was a big bugger. Jimmy said quietly, "I could take ye roun some time. I could say ye're ma sister an get ye in for free. Take ye aff the road, right up close tae the lions an that."

10

"Could ye?" Her eyes were wide open. "I'd love that."

Later, when he went for a piss, Iain followed him into the gents. "Listen," he said, "juist in case ye wis thinkin about it, keep your fuckin paws aff Carol, aa right?"

"Hey, I'm juist out for a bevvy," said Jimmy.

"Ye think ye're somethin special, you an Eck," said Iain. "Workin out at that glorified zoo. Carol said ye were gaunae show her roun. Well, ye might fool her but ye dinna fool me. Tae me ye're juist a pair o jumped-up sheepshaggers."

"Hell, man," said Jimmy as he went to wash his hands, "I ken ye lost at pool but dinna tak it out on me, aa right?"

Behind him he heard Iain moving. He turned round quickly, expecting to have to fight, but Iain was heading for the door. Probably going to check on what Eck was up to with Carol. Jimmy shook his hands dry. Time for them to move on to the next pub. The woman must not have a brain, telling Iain that. He'd be as well staying clear of her.

Jimmy understood that the Park was a charade, but he resented a guy like Iain who knew fuck all about it criticising it. You shouldn't criticise things you knew nothing about. What was it he'd said? A glorified zoo? What would that be? A zoo without cages. Ah, well, he would know about that right enough. They all would.

When Murray came back with the monkey he found he had a bigger problem on his hands. Eilidh had to lie crumpled up in the stall all day—there was no way she could be moved with the public around. After the Park closed, Murray got Jimmy and Eck and a couple of others to stay on so they could shift her.

"Where's she gaun?" asked Jimmy.

"Doun tae the mink ferm," said Murray, "where else? Eck, you can get on tae it the morn's morn."

While Gav was backing the trailer in Jimmy said to Eck, "Whit's he on about? He's surely no wantin ye tae cut her up?"

"Dinna ken, Jim," said Eck. He wouldn't look Jimmy in the eye.

"Christ, man, she's fuckin rife wi gangrene. She should be

gaun in the incinerator, no bein fed tae the lions."

"I'll tak a look at her the morn," said Eck. "Nou piss aff. I've things tae think about."

That was odd. Eck had never deliberately had a thought in his life, to Jimmy's knowledge. Now apparently he was having several at once.

Jimmy never saw him all the next morning, which meant he was probably at the mink farm. On his dinner hour Jimmy jumped on the bike and hammered it down there. He found Eck in the big rubber apron, holding a long knife and surveying Eilidh, who was stretched out on the concrete floor of the meat-room. But it wasn't the Eilidh Jimmy knew. This was Eilidh in her socks just. All the skin was stripped off her apart from four wee socks above her hooves. Her severed head lay on the floor a few feet away. The flayed corpse was bloody and stinking, parts of the meat were a grey-green colour. "You were right," said Eck, "there's nae wey the cats can eat this. We'd kill the lot o them."

"So whit's the idea?"

"The idea *wis*," said Eck, "tae sell the skin. It's worth quite a few bob if ye can tak it aff in a oner. Trouble is, wi that wound she had, there a fuckin great hole in it. Nae bluidy use at aa." He had the skin stretched out on the floor, and had been scraping bits of meat and gunge off it. Now he began to cover the inner side of it with handfuls of salt from a big sack, rolling the skin up and rubbing the salt well into it, packing the skin into a tight bundle.

"So whit's aa this for?"

"Murray wants it."

"Murray wants it?"

"Ay. How? It's nae big deal."

"It's obscene."

"How? She's deid. Nae sense in wastin it. Canna sell it wi thon big hole in it, so Murray says he'll hae it."

"Whit for?"

"How dae I ken? For his house, probably. For his front room. Hey, imagine his new chat-up line. 'Right, doll, want tae come back tae ma place an make love in front o a big roarin fire on ma giraffe?'"

Jimmy laughed. "He could have one end at the fire an the ither ablow the jawbox in his kitchen. So they could wash up efter an no get their feet cauld."

"It'd be great for a lobby-runner," said Eck.

Eilidh's guts were piled up in a heap on a big flat board. Eck said, "Here, this stuff weighs a ton. Gaunae gie me a haun tae lift it in the skip?"

Between them they dragged the board out of the meat-room and over to the skip which doubled as an incinerator. Getting it up to shoulder-level was hard, the guts shifting their bulk around on the board. But they managed to heave it over the edge and let Eilidh's entrails slide down into the bottom of the skip. They landed on top of a wee monkey corpse.

The smell was very bad. Eck chucked in some diesel and half an old bale of straw and put a match to it. "I fun a deid dug in here last week," he said as they backed away from the stench. "Some fowk've nae respect."

Then he said, "Listen, Murray doesna ken this yet. He's gaunae go mental when he finds out, in case onybody else does an he gets the blame for no lookin efter her properly. Eilidh wis pregnant."

He took Jimmy through the meat-room to a second, smaller room at the back. On the concrete floor lay a miniature version of the skinless Eilidh, eighteen perfect inches from head to tail. The neck was curved and graceful even in death. There were two round swellings which would have been the eyes. The delicate, tiny trotters—they weren't big enough to be called hooves— were already formed. The pink skin had a pattern of red lines beneath it, outlining just where the brown and white patches of the coat would have grown.

"A while tae go yet," said Eck. "I cut it away frae the sack. It might no hae lived—wi Eilidh bein how she wis—but it looks healthy enough tae me. Funny, did ye ever see the male shaggin her? If we'd kent about this the vet might hae wanted Eilidh treated different."

"I didna think the male had a shag left in him," said Jimmy. "Murray should hae kent, but. The fuckin vet inspected her—he should hae noticed."

"Murray kens fuck aa about animals," said Eck. "He's nae fuckin empathy wi them at aa. If he could get away wi it he'd be as bad as fuckin Maxton. An the vet's a fuckin waster. I tell ye, Jimmy, you an me are mair in tune wi the fuckin animals in this Park, you an me feedin them ither animals, than the fuckin so-called management."

Jimmy always thought Eck had something on Murray, some kind of hold on him. It just shows how wrong you can be. Eck must have tried it on too hard with the Eilidh thing—maybe Murray felt threatened with what Eck knew about it. Well, anyway, he called Eck's bluff. Two weeks after the skinning of Eilidh, Murray drove down the mink farm road one afternoon, switched off his motor two hundred yards short, coasted in and caught Eck kipping in the hay with a Louis L'Amour book over his face. First warning. Eck should have realised then that Murray was after him, he should have been on his guard. But Eck wasn't like that, he couldn't wise up. Within the week Murray had hauled him up for not cleaning out the meat-room properly, being late in for work again, and taking an extra ten minutes on his dinner. That was the one that finished it. "I'm sittin on the pan," says Eck to Jimmy in the pub that weekend, "I'm sittin there evacuatin the premises afore gettin back tae ma work,"—he was covering for Jimmy that day at the giraffe-house, it being Jimmy's day off—"an the cunt comes in an haimmers on the door. 'Is that you in there, Eck?' 'Ay, Murray,' I says, 'I'm juist digestin ma dinner.' 'Well,' he says, 'when ye've digested that, digest this: ye're fired. Ye can get your buiks at the office.' 'Aw come on, Murray,' I says but he juist batters on, 'Dinna fuckin argue wi me, Eck Galbraith, I've had enough o your fuckin mouth.' Then I hear him on his radio calling the office, so every other bastart with a radio can hear him. 'Mary,' he says, 'Mary, will you make up Hector Galbraith's wages, whatever he's due, he's finishing up the-day. He'll be along for them in twenty minutes.' The bastart. He says, 'Oh, Mary, mind and take off the ten-pound sub he owes us.' I'm stuck on the pan cursin him for aa I'm worth an he juist goes, 'Wipe your airse, Eck. I dout I've wiped the smirk aff your face aaready.'"

And that was Eck. He'd been there as long as anyone could mind. Jimmy still sees him when he goes for a beer sometimes, but it's different: Eck works behind the bar in the Red Lion. He doesn't take a drink when he's on duty and he doesn't like talking about the Park. Jimmy left of his own accord, a year later, and got a job with the Post Office. One time in the pub Jimmy said, "D'ye mind the day Eilidh died?" but Eck just looked at him and said, "Whit about it?" so Jimmy said, "Doesna maitter, Eck." But Jimmy minds it all right, and so does Eck.

Four days after Eck was fired, Murray remembered about the meat-room, how there was nobody looking after it any more. The lions and tigers were needing fed again. This time they'd no choice—they had to haul some sheep out of the freezer and hope for the best. This was because of the state of the meat-room—nobody had touched it since Eck went, and it was near the end of May. That summer was a hot one—not as hot as 'seventy-six, but it was doing its damnedest. Murray sent Jimmy Sanderson and Dave Maxton down to clean up.

When they pulled the big sliding-door back at first they didn't understand what it was falling on their heads. Then the smell hit them and they understood. The floor, the walls, the door were crawling with maggots, big fat white bastards like polystyrene chips that exploded when you stepped on them. In the middle of the floor, where it dipped down towards the drain, lay a heap of wool and decomposing meat that had once been three or maybe four sheep, it was hard to tell. It was oozing black blood and heaving with maggots and cockroaches. The pair of them backed out gagging, shaking and slapping at their heads.

"I'm no fuckin daein this," said Maxton. "Get on the radio tae Murray an tell him we're no fuckin daein it."

Jimmy held the radio out to him. "On ye go, Dave," he said.

15

"You tell him." He knew they'd be doing it. They both knew. If Murray could get rid of Eck he could get rid of anybody. That was it really. They were stuck. They didn't have great prospects in front of them. They had to take what they were given.

The Plagues

This is a dream Leonard once had:

Seven fat cows come up out of the river to graze. Then come seven lean cows, all skin stretched on bone. They come out of the river and they eat up the fat cows.

What did it mean?

It was odd because it was a boss's dream, a rich man's dream, and Leonard was not rich. It was someone else's dream that had somehow found its way into Leonard's head. There was fear in the dream, and guilt.

Also, it was a warning, which a rich man would probably ignore.

Years later. Leonard had a job but not because he could interpret the boss's dreams. He worked in a bookshop, behind the till. But he didn't do dreams, the boss's or anybody else's. It was enough to cope with his own. That is, if they were dreams at all, which he doubted.

It was this problem with the frogs. In the past they had never used to bother him because he couldn't see them, but lately they'd been appearing everywhere. It wasn't as if he hadn't always known they were there, waiting, but for a long time they were quite invisible to him. If he spent the evening at home, they stayed out of sight. He knew they were moving behind the plaster of the walls, or down in the street, or congregating in unimaginable numbers in the canal, but they were impossible to see. If he went out, though, well—as soon as his back was turned they would emerge. He would be walking down the street on his way to the pub, and a black taxi, seemingly empty but with its For Hire light off, would pass him before he had gone four hundred yards. Below the level of its windows it would be loaded with frogs, ready to pour out and occupy the flat until his return. Parked cars that he passed would be teeming with the buggers, but if he looked through their windows he would see nothing, all would be still. He remembered a poem from his childhood about walking the pavement and how the bears would get you if you stepped on the lines. Walking to the pub was like that, only with frogs. They were too quick and too numerous for him, but he knew they were there. And now, lately, they'd been getting bolder. They didn't hide from him as they once had. He'd hoped he would get used to them, but it was impossible when they were in such numbers. He couldn't help being anxious about them. Anyone would be in his position.

Not that he had anything against frogs in themselves. Until recently, when they'd become such an overwhelming presence, he would have gone so far as to say that the idea of them always appealed to him. He remembered something else from his childhood. Every spring and summer he would go to a loch in the hills behind the town where his family stayed, in search of frogs. It might take two or three visits, but he always found them. Year after year they would be there—and so would he. Thinking back, he reckoned the loch must have been an important breeding-ground. At a certain time in the spring hundreds of frogs gathered under the banks in a kind of mass orgy. For a while after that, there would be nothing except the spawn filled with black life-dots, sago lapping in the weeds. Then, one day, he would go up there and find that the spawn had turned to tadpoles, and that the tadpoles were changing too, and all around the loch tiny frogs, no bigger than his thumbnail, were leaving the water. Thousands upon thousands of them. The track around the loch was so thickly covered that he could not avoid treading on them with every step he took. And if the sun was out and the day hot, hundreds of their tiny bodies, dehydrated and blackened, would be stretched on the grass and rocks. It was suicide for them to be moving away from the water on such a day, but it seemed that they could not help themselves, they moved away relentlessly, driven by something of which they had no knowledge or understanding.

These were the circumstances of his youth. He would even

say he loved the frogs then. They were helpless, fragile, and yet their numbers seemed a source of strength. Enough would survive to return the following year and participate in a fresh orgy of procreation. Yes, he loved the frogs, and the other creatures of the loch; the heron, the pair of swans which returned every spring to breed, the ducks, the rabbits, the stoats. There was a sense of unison, of reassurance in the inevitable circles of nature, and he could sit for hours, or wander slowly around the water, and feel a great energy surrounding him even though he himself might be lazy and listless. But now it was different. Now he was disturbed by frogs. Not those ones, the long vanished amphibians of his childhood. Those were good frogs, country frogs. It was the others that were the trouble, the ones that had come to the city, that were always with him, ever present.

Leonard's job also caused him anxiety. All day long people kept coming to him with these packages. They handed him the packages and he put them in a bag and they gave him money for them. He put the money in the till and gave them the bag and their change and a receipt and they went away. It kept happening.

The packages were all very similar. They were rectangular, full of little black squiggles and lines. Most of them were about six inches by four, and about half an inch thick. Some were much bigger and some smaller, some were hard, others flexible, but really they were all much alike. Although they had different pictures on the front and lines on the back explaining what the packages contained, inside they looked the same. Usually there was some truth in the explanations, sometimes they were utter lies. Leonard knew this because he himself had inspected many of the packages, every sheet that was in them and, what was more, in the right order.

Sometimes he thought—perhaps I need my head examined. A person undertaking such an examination would say, how can you be a bookseller and have such an attitude to books? (That, plus the frogs nonsense.) This is not soap-powder you are selling, it is Literature. Ah, he would retort, you literati always turn snooty when it comes to soap-powder. And yet it serves a definite and worthy function. You don't find people buying a packet of soap-powder and taking it home and staring at it for hours on end in front of the fire. The people who came into the bookshop, they did this with the packages they selected. They sought enlightenment or reassurance or excitement from the conglomeration of wood-pulp and glue and ink in their lap. Leonard knew, he used to do it himself. These days he didn't believe the packages contained anything as useful as soap-powder.

One thing about the frogs. It wasn't just him. He used to think it was, but then he began to see it in other people's eyes. That haunted, nervous look. You didn't get like that unless the frogs were bothering you. Of course people tried to stay calm, pretend everything was normal. That was what he did. But sometimes he looked into another face and he knew it was happening there too. Well, it stood to reason really. All these frogs and only being seen by the one person, it just wasn't credible. Sooner or later, he supposed, somebody was going to have the courage to mention them, and then they'd all start. What do you think's causing it? We must be doing something bad, that's why it's happening. We're going against nature. We're holding people under duress. He'd have said something himself but he didn't like to be the first. It might be dangerous. If the frogs thought you were about to squeal they might make a move on you, take you out. And he didn't want to speak too soon and find that nobody else had got that worried. Yet. He didn't want to jump the gun.

This Literature business. In order to disabuse yourself of the notion that the art of writing is somehow elevated, refined or other-worldly, visit a printer's or the distribution centre of a large publisher. Leonard went to such a place once in connection with his work in the bookshop. There he did indeed see Literature reduced and diminished. Cursing drivers fork-lifted

20

pallets of Shakespeare as though it were dogfood; men covered in sweat and tattoos, their arms dipped to the elbows in grease, operated machines that cut, mashed and pummelled the packages, with not a thought as to their contents. Ernest Hemingway was ruthlessly shrinkwrapped, Virginia Woolf glued and bound; yesterday's hopeful new writers were dispatched *en masse* to the pulp chambers. It became evident to him there that against violence all those squiggles and lines were quite powerless.

Things got out of control one afternoon in May, in the shop. He wasn't feeling too well—slightly nauseous and light-headed. Outside it was raining and the trouble came from there, in out of the wet. He didn't see it come in but that was the logical source. Also there was a thin pallid young man carrying a large empty sports-bag. He had to be watched. And a middle-aged, well-to-do woman shaking her umbrella and demanding attention. She came up to the till and said:

"Do you have that new one by the Balmoral chambermaid?"

Leonard was shaping a reply to her in his head when everything started happening at once. The thin man, who had gone to the horror section, unzipped his sports-bag and began to load it with paperback packages. The woman said, "Because if you have I should warn you that I shall never shop here again." And a sudden green movement at the edge of his vision caused Leonard to look over at the fiction shelves, where round about the Wilbur Smiths a small single frog perched for a fleeting moment before disappearing with a sideways spring.

"Excuse me one moment," he said to the woman, keeping his eyes fixed on the spot. He didn't feel under an obligation to her anyway as she'd asked a trick question. "A slight emergency has arisen." This was an under-statement. It was the first time he had ever seen a frog in the shop. He took a magazine from the counter and rolled it up to make a weapon. The weapon he made was a knobkerrie, a round-headed stick used as a club and missile by natives of southern Africa. He began to move cautiously towards the shelves.

"Whatever is the matter?" the woman demanded. "Will you

answer my question?"

"Please be quiet," Leonard said. "You'll disturb it." He could cope with them at home—just about—and on the outside. But here, in his place of work—this was a new development. He took a risk and glanced at the woman. It was obvious from her eyes that the frogs had not yet entered her life.

It was tricky. The thief was stacking the horror packages into his bag very neatly and efficiently, as if they were small bricks. But the priority was definitely the frog.

He was halfway to the fiction shelves when the woman said very loudly, "Where is the Manager?"

"A good question," said Leonard. "I should like to know. I think it went in behind the Ps."

"This is deplorable," said the woman. "I refuse to wait a minute longer."

"Be patient," he said to her, still advancing step by step. "They're not like mice, you know. You can't just set traps for them."

Possibly she might have responded, but at this point things took a turn for the worse. The thief, who was returning from the horror shelves with a further selection, let out a cry and dropped the pile he was holding. His open-mouthed stare swung back and forth between Leonard and his knobkerrie and the half-filled bag. From where Leonard was, it was possible to see the sides of the bag rippling and bulging. The thief backed away with his hand to his mouth.

"Oh my God," said Leonard. It was a trap. He started to shout, holding his weapon aloft. "Get back! Everybody back!" The woman retreated. Leonard could feel the sweat breaking out on his face. He wasn't sure what was happening, if the damage could be limited. He wanted to say something reassuring like, "Everybody please leave the premises in an orderly fashion," but both the angry woman and the frightened thief had already gone.

Leonard made it back to the counter and pressed the buzzer for assistance. He was breathing heavily and felt very hot. The Manager arrived in a hurry. "What happened?" he asked. "You look dreadful." Leonard tried to explain. "This woman didn't want to buy a package if we had it," he said. "I don't feel well. And look, there's a bag over there but you mustn't touch it. You'll have to phone for the frog disposal squad."

"I don't know what you're talking about," said the Manager. This was only to be expected. He reached for the knobkerrie. "Stop waving that about before you do yourself an injury, poke your eye out or something." The Manager came to a decision. "Leonard, I'm calling a taxi to take you home." Appalling! He couldn't possibly get in a taxi. "It's fine," he said. "I mean, I'm fine. No I'm not. I'll walk. Get a bus, I mean. Honestly, the fresh air will help."

Outside the sun was coming out. The pavements were beginning to steam. Leonard walked along briskly, determined to get home before the next attack. Black cabs swept past him. He tried to get his mind around the possibilities.

What was it all about? This was what people were bound to ask: what was it about? This was what they were always asking. But what did they want to know? Did they want him to tell them what it meant, or what he thought it meant? How could he do that? It might not mean anything. He could tell them only what he believed.

He believed that all the margins of his life were smitten with frogs. They came out of the rivers and drains and out of the old canal beside the street where he lived, and they got everywhere—in the house, in the bedroom, in the bed itself. He opened the oven and they were there, and they sat green and sullen in the saucepans and baking-trays in the cupboard below the sink. They were in the fridge and the washing-machine and there were a couple of dead ones in the toaster and they got down the sides of the armchairs and into the cupboard where he kept his videos and they sat like little green ornaments on the window-ledges. And in the bathroom, that was the worst, it was overrun with them, they climbed the shower-curtain and squatted on the soap and left their traces all over the surface of the bath and basin, and they came in clusters up through the toilet. And he dreaded that they would come upon his person, into his

23

clothes and hair, whether he was asleep or awake. This was an awful anticipation.

But, more than this, he feared the aftermath, when the summer came and the sun burnt them up and he would be able to sweep them into the street and reclaim his own territory. He could already see the piles of corpses in the streets, he could catch the first whiff of their stench. And this was only the frogs. He knew there was worse, much worse, to come.

Screen Lives

She was home.

Her clothes still smelt of suntan oil. Her hair retained the thick heavy feel of swimming in the sea, drying in the sun, and with her nail she could still pick a few grains of sand from her scalp. Other parts of her body also, even after a couple of days, retained that salt scent and texture. For example, she loved to nuzzle deep into the crook of her arm and breathe in the beach and the sea, gently rub the soft brown crease with the tip of her nose and let her eye rest, unfocused, on the bleached hairs of her arm, her mind away.

But she was home. Dark Shona beginning to fade again, until next year. There was no escaping that.

Her first morning back at work she chose to wear dark colours. She had toyed with the idea of white, but she didn't want the others to think she was showing off her tan. Of course she wanted them to comment on it—she was almost black in places—but she didn't want them thinking that was all her holiday consisted of, just soaking up the sun for two weeks, thoughtless.

On her way to the bus-stop some men putting up scaffolding on a block of flats whistled and cheered at her. She kept her head down, angry and embarrassed. She knew she was supposed also to be secretly pleased, but she wasn't. She had never felt flattered by the attentions of such men; the stupidity and crudeness depressed and frightened her. These ones were putting in a lot of effort. It must be the tan, showing on her legs beneath her short skirt. That was all she was showing.

In Crete she had gone topless on the beach, and if anyone had been eyeing her up they didn't let on by shouting and whistling.

Most of the women were topless. In fact it was the few who weren't that you noticed. All sizes and shapes of breast acquired a normality that was, after all, only normal. Even the men didn't seem to bother. Sometimes, though, she found herself looking at the other women, comparing. She liked her own breasts best. Lying with her back to the sun and resting on her elbows while she read a book, she cradled them between her arms, moving herself forward so that the nipples brushed against her forearms. Then she would find that she hadn't been reading the words in the book at all, and that her nipples were hard and wanting, and she would have to lie flat for a while, pressing her body into the towel and the beach below, blanking the ache from her mind.

A hook had lain in the pit of her stomach, gently goading her, sickening her, but now she thought she could feel it beginning to unbend and soften. For months her life had been in limbo. She had become aware of her dissatisfaction, but instead of trying to identify the source she had waited, as if for inspiration. She was waiting for her life to change.

Then one day she woke up and realised it would not happen. Something could come over your life, a mood, a feeling, but it had to be acted upon. Otherwise it simply weighed you down, daring you and subduing you at once.

She would never know what came first—this mood of disenchantment, or Devlin. Devlin had crept up on her too—he was no vision appearing suddenly, blinding her with love. In fact she hadn't even liked him much, to begin with. When she started working there she remarked upon his name—was it Irish, she wondered—and he said, "It's after the character in *Notorious*—you know, the old Hitchcock film?" She nodded, of course she knew it, and he went on, "My mother loved Cary Grant and my father loved Ingrid Bergman, so I suppose if I'd been a girl I'd be Alicia. It could be worse, I could have been a football team." But he said it in such a practised manner that she thought, you think you are Cary Grant, don't you, you smug bastard. Even though he didn't look in the least bit like him, he was fair and a little

26

ungainly, not smooth at all.

So probably it started not with Devlin but with the mood, within herself. But she could never be sure.

Or it might have been George. She was not so self-centred as to assume that change came only to her alone. George too was changing. They'd been going out for a year, long enough to breed boredom, not so long that she was afraid to let go.

So this day came when she woke up and decided to act. In the evening she phoned George. It was cowardly but she didn't want to face him. She didn't want a scene. "George, I want to stop seeing you." "George, I don't want to go on seeing you." She rehearsed the two lines, wondering which was better, more truthful.

It didn't matter. She didn't use either, and he didn't fight about it. She said, "George, I feel things have changed. I don't think there's much point in us going on with each other." He agreed. This made her more certain that she was doing the right thing, that he too was changing. If he had fought to keep her, she might have had doubts. But he just said, "All right." It would have been hurtful if she had felt differently: she wasn't important to him after all. And so he passed out of her life, almost as if he had never been there.

But what if one person changed and the other didn't? That was when things became truly awful. What if this happened to married people—as it did—people who had grown so accustomed to one another that if one changed it was like tearing a chunk out of the other? The very thought of such trouble made her feel sick and weak.

And then she got over thinking he was too smart. Devlin. They made each other laugh. There was a cheap reissue of *Notorious* on video, and she bought a copy and watched it through. The lines and the shots came back to her just before they happened, so that they arrived like old friends. She watched it again the next night, understanding what a great, almost perfect film it was. In the morning she wanted to show off her appreciation to him, so when he came on the internal phone to her she contrived to interrupt him: "What's your name? What's your name?" She heard his voice, surprised, a little offended perhaps, say, "It's Devlin, Shona," and then she hit him with it: "Well, you showed that cop something and he saluted you. . . . Why, you double-crossing buzzard, you're a cop!" The joke was over-constructed but he got it, he laughed. After that they both began to work it into every conversation, trying to outdo one another. He'd come to her office and say, "We've got a problem here," and she'd break into it, saying, "What's the matter? Don't look so tense," and he wouldn't say anything, just stare moodily out of the window, so she'd go on, "Look, I'll make it easy for you: the time has come when you must tell me that you have a wife and two adorable children and this madness between us can't go on any longer." Then, he'd say, "I bet you've heard that line often enough," and she'd say, "Right below the belt every time," and he'd break it off saying, "Actually, it's this contract, it needs to be redrafted." Or she'd be coming down with the flu and he'd say, "You don't look so hot. Sick?" And she'd muster a smile even though she felt dreadful, and say, "No. Hangover," and he'd say, "That's news. Back on the bottle again." It was funny, and nobody else could join in, because it was just them, Cary and Ingrid. It was romantic. They both laughed but it was romantic. They were living out the movie.

After she had spoken to George she phoned her sister Louise. For the last three years they had gone on holiday together. She had been going to break the habit this year—she had been going to go with George—but now she phoned her to discuss destinations. They settled on Crete. They had always gone for islands: the Canaries, Corfu, Corsica, and now Crete.

She felt weak at the thought of trouble between lovers, yet she was not weak. She was deliberately reshaping her life, and she was pushing herself into a phase of it that might very well involve pain and more frustration. For she did not really know if Devlin would respond to her or if she would dare to make a move. Her change was not necessarily his at all. It would be like self-inflicted torture to have him in her thoughts all the time like this, if in fact he was not changing with her, to her. But surely he was—there were too many looks and smiles for her to have misread? And all the time he *was* in her thoughts. She imagined herself doing the most outrageous, beautiful things to him, her body to his, her mouth on him, his hands on her. She shocked herself with what she would do. There was in fact nothing she would *not* do!

Was it wrong to think of someone like that? It wasn't guilt that made her ask that question, but real concern. It was like an invasion, using someone against their will, or at least without their knowledge. There were social rules as to how you should treat another person, how you had to have their consent—but in your imagination these rules did not apply. You could do anything to them, anything. You could make love to them, or you could hurt them. If you hated them enough, you could even kill them. But mostly, she thought, it must be love. A person had one life, but in the minds of other people they could have more. Dozens, perhaps. Thousands, in the case of someone famous. How many lovers did Cary Grant and Ingrid Bergman have, that they knew nothing about?

Someone you knew. You knew them at your work, or as a friend of a friend. And you made love to them without their knowledge. Did you take something from them when this happened? Could you capture a part of them as they had captured you?

In Crete she slept with a waiter from the hotel, a beautiful boy who was always in a loose white shirt, on duty or off, cool in his white shirt and moving with the grace of a cat and with soft thick black hair like a cat's. Probably he had a different girl every two weeks, as often as the package flights arrived and departed, but she didn't care. (She was careful, but she didn't care.) It was as if he were part of the holiday, an extra hidden in the small print of the brochure. Louise scoffed at her—going with a waiter was so *naff*—but he took them both to the best clubs and introduced

29

them to the barmen so that they got their drinks cheap or even free, so she didn't complain too much. All she wanted to do was dance, dance, dance—with Shona, with guys, it didn't matter—it was as if she was dancing to push everything else in her life to the edges of her consciousness. The dancing was all. Shona's waiter said he could fix Louise up with one of his friends but Shona said, no, she's happy, she only wants to dance. *Her* life wasn't changing, at least it didn't look like it. She lived constantly in the present, never thinking either side of whatever three-minute song was playing. All day on the beach she slept. She didn't even go in the sea.

Ingrid: "I'm practically on the wagon, that's quite a change."
Cary: "It's a phase."
Ingrid: "You don't think a woman can change?"
Cary: "Sure. A change is fun. For a while."
Ingrid: "For a while."

The trouble was, Devlin was attached. He lived with someone. She knew this of course but she couldn't help herself. Maybe that was where he and her change of mood came together, because she would hardly have begun to think of him in that way, the way that brought on the ache, if he had not one day, in one of their good conversations together, taken her into his confidence and talked about the relationship, explained that it was all but over. So he too was experiencing change. And they *did* have good conversations at work—but mostly *about* work, or about the news, or flippant, jokey banter about anything at all—good conversations that suggested even better ones, deep serious ones in other places and long into the night in which they could come to know each other completely. Conversations which would perhaps eventually die away because there would no longer be any need to speak, only to touch, only this deep need to touch.

"It's good to see you," he said, halfway through the morning. "And you're looking fantastic. That's some tan!"

"Did you miss me, then?" she said. She asked it lightly, but there was just so much weight in it.

"Of course I missed you," he replied, and it seemed to her that he balanced the weight exactly.

"How are things?" Again, she asked it as casually as she could, but he looked at her in just such a way, and it was obvious he knew what she meant. Things at home. He said, "Pretty bad still, I suppose." And she said, "But you're sorting something out, aren't you? You're doing something about it?" And he said, "Yes, but it's not easy."

"It won't happen itself," she said. She was certain about this now, and certain that he would understand. She had this new knowledge inside her, from her own experience. She wanted to set him free too. "I know," he said.

Later she said, "Let's go for a drink after work. Come out and talk to me?" The way she looked at him. She could hardly believe she was being so forward. And neither, apparently, could he. She saw that she had pushed too hard, that he shied away from her, wincing as if she had touched a wound.

"Better not," he said. "Not tonight. Maybe some other time. Sorry. I just wouldn't be good company."

It was an awkward moment. She said, to cover it over, "It's stuffy in here, isn't it?" Her Bergman voice.

"Might be," he said, mustering Cary. She slurred the next line:

"What about . . . we have a picnic."

"Outside?"

"It's too stuffy in here for a picnic."

He smiled at her, that wounded smile that seemed to be conceding victory to her in some game, and left her at her desk, the cursor on her screen flashing impatiently, midway through a sentence. She sat and stared at the green oblong flashing faster than the seconds going by, hating its insistent demand on her time.

And yes, time was passing. It seemed now that it was going by very fast indeed. Suddenly she was afraid. She was fading

31

away—more, much more than just her stupid tan. She looked at the screen, half-expecting to see the text vanish in front of her eyes. She put her fingers to her throat and found a fold of skin under her jaw, slack like the skin of an old woman. She plucked at it, filled with a terrible dread of being old, of not having done all these things. It was not death that she feared, but waiting for death. All she wanted, all she had ever wanted, was to be alive.

The Jonah

Billy was on the road, at the edge of it. Shoulders hunched, he waited for something to come out of the mist at him. The rain crept cold fingers down his back. Every so often he sneaked a look over his upturned collar, hoping for a car, lorry, tractor, push-chair—anything that might move them on a few miles. He had been doing this for a long time. It was hard to stay philosophical about it.

A few feet away Sean hawked and gobbed on the tarmac. Billy heard the splat even through the rain. He heard Sean swear at the weather. If he was expecting sympathy he could forget it. It was Sean's fault they were stuck where they were and cursing the rain wasn't going to get them out. Only some total stranger with space in his motor for two men and their rucksacks was going to do that. They'd been waiting long enough—nearly two hours since the last cup of tea—and Sean's patience was exhausted, but Billy's trust still clung to the cliff-face of fate. Fate would have someone organised. Even now they'd be tootling along, oblivious to their role in Billy's life, maybe just a few miles to the south. In all the years Billy had hitch-hiked around, home or abroad, he had never not got a lift eventually. He might have been stuck for whole days in some places but he'd always escaped in the end, and this was going to be no exception. Not unless Sean turned out to be some kind of hitch-hiker's Jonah. Billy had never hitched with him before so he couldn't tell. But his attitude was all wrong, and attitude was important if you were going to hitch successfully. You had to do it with optimism, and faith in human nature. You had to have a belief in the logic of coincidences. Positive fatalism. That wasn't Sean at all. He didn't think on the big scale like Billy. He didn't see connections. He just stumbled around life, banging his head and treading on toes. Sean all over.

33

And yet he had something, Billy had to concede that. He had the power of persuasion. For example, he'd managed to persuade Billy off course into this vehicle-forsaken hole in darkest Perthshire—or was it still Stirlingshire?—and Billy, the one supposedly with the plan, had fallen for it. He might never have hitched with Sean before but he'd been around him off and on for years and he still hadn't learned his lesson: it was very hard to say no to him. Correction: saying no to him didn't make any difference.

They were headed for pastures new. Forests new. That was the idea. Their old forestry pal Kenny McPhail had beckoned them. He'd phoned Billy at his ma's house one night from somewhere in the northwest. Billy imagined him there, digging for coins in his jeans pocket, he could see the solitary phone-box at the junction of two single-track roads. "Get your arses up here fast," Kenny said. "I've spoken to the gaffer about yous and if you can get here for Tuesday there's a good chance of a whole summer's work." A whole summer taking out a semi-mature plantation. Billy smelt the foustiness of old rucksacks, the dampness of mouse-ridden caravans. He said, "The both of us?" and Kenny said, "Ay, but tell that bawheid Sean he's got to behave himself this time. Nae skiving on the job and that." "I'll tell him," said Billy. "Listen," said Kenny, "better hurry before every other bastard and his dog turns up. That's my money gone now. I've put the word in for yous so you'll be all right, but try and get here by Tuesday. Wednesday at the—"

That was Saturday and this was Monday. Two whole days just to go three hundred miles and they'd only managed about sixty so far. Sean was to blame, chasing non-existent women all over the country and dragging Billy along with him. He had no idea about responsibility, and as for urgency the only time he ever felt a sense of it was if he was taking his breeks off to get his end away.

They'd got in a carry-out on the Saturday night—it was cheaper than going to the pub—and decided what to do. Billy's mind was already made up—he was going after Kenny. He'd been taking it easy for too long, signing on, picking up a few bob on the side working for a guy who did house removals. "I need to make some real money," he said.

"I'm no sure," said Sean. "I mean, if you're going up there anyway, I could stick around. Andro'd be wanting somebody else to help him on the van, just a few hours a week like, but it's all in the hand."

"Ay," said Billy, "whereas in the bush. . . ." They laughed. Sean had this old proverb he liked to trot out: "A push in the bush is worth two hand-jobs." "Ya fucking robot," he said now. "No, but," said Billy, "working for Andro's all right, but it's no the same as a wage, is it, even after paying the tax."

It wasn't about money for Sean, it was about a lassie. Billy knew this. She was nineteen years old—six years younger than Sean—and he'd been seeing her for three weeks, a record for him. Billy could see that this was the problem, even though Sean wasn't admitting it.

"It's that Susan Donovan, isn't it?"

"Eh? Fuck off!"

"Ay it is. Her with the three big brothers."

"What's that supposed to mean?"

"Nothing. Just, you fancy a shotgun wedding, do ye?"

"How? She's no up the pole."

"She might be, with your methods. Or lack of them."

"Fuck off!"

"Fine. It's your funeral—I mean, wedding."

Sean and Billy had these arguments, about contraception and that. Sean wouldn't use anything. Said if the woman wanted to, that was up to her, but he wasn't sticking one of thae bloody things on. What about AIDS, Billy would say. Sean said, "I don't go with junkies and I'm no a poof." But now Billy could see he'd set him thinking, about the number of times he'd done it with Susan Donovan, who probably didn't use anything either, and after about a minute he said, "Right, let's go the morn."

Between them they had enough money for a bit more bevvy and food to get them up the road, maybe enough for a B&B if they couldn't make it in one day. It never occurred to them to do anything other than hitch. That was part of the whole thing, taking off up north. Bugger the bus—full of tourists and drunk teuchters. And then Sean said about wanting to go up the west side, he knew these two women that were spending the summer waitressing in some fishing hotel and he wanted to drop in on them, take them by surprise like, meet them after they got off duty, charm them onto their backs and shag them senseless. "A fitting start to this new chapter in our lives, Billy," he said. "Your brain's in your Y-fronts," said Billy, but he was stupid enough to go along with it, he was that pleased with himself for getting Sean away from Susan without so much as a goodbye. Which was why they'd spent the previous night getting plastered in a hotel bar miles off the main road—"This is definitely the place," Sean kept saying, "I know this is the place, I'm sure this is the place"—until finally they were so drunk they had to book into the place—twenty pound each for a twin room and breakfast. . . . It would have been daylight robbery if it hadn't been nearly midnight.

Billy needed the work. They both did, but Billy was determined this was going to be more than just another chapter. If there really was three or four months' work to get out of the job he was going to be disciplined about it. He was going to save money. If that meant staying in the camp or B&B or wherever they were going to be instead of getting bevvied every night, even if it made him unpopular with the rest of the crew, so be it. If they were being put up in a hotel he wouldn't go near the bar. He would read books, listen to his Walkman, write letters, wank (play the free one-armed bandit, as Sean put it), anything to save money. If he could put a few hundred away, a thousand maybe, enough to get the airfare anyway, then he was going to Australia. He knew a guy who'd done it two years ago. Once he was past immigration he'd just disappeared, invented a few names and national insurance numbers and hopped around from job to job for eighteen months. The money he earned was unbelievable. Thousands and thousands of dollars he made. Right enough when he finally left the country he got a black mark against his name, would probably never get back in, and right enough too he'd spent all the money when he got home again and wasn't working now, but Billy wasn't going to make the same mistake. He was going to work himself into the ground out there, pocket the money, then come back and buy himself a nice wee flat somewhere. Nowhere he was known. Glasgow or some place big enough to get lost in. Well, it would have to be Glasgow then, if he was going to get lost in Scotland. Or Dundee, he'd never been there in his life, nobody knew him in Dundee. Buy a place, cash down, no mortgage shite or nothing, and then never work again. Or just enough to pay the bills. Work at will. No more wage-slavery. If you had a paid-for roof over your head and nobody depending on you you didn't need much in the way of an income. And he had enough skills to pick up work and drop it again as it suited him. Things were bad but they weren't so bad that Billy couldn't find himself something if he needed it enough.

But all that was hanging on him getting this job, and right at the moment the possibility of failure had to be admitted, the possibility of not getting there in time. No, wrong attitude. That was the mindset of the Seans of the world. Wouldn't do at all.

"It's going to need a fucking miracle for somebody to stop for us here," said Sean.

"It's going to need a miracle for anybody to be on this road. So if there is, they'll stop for us."

"Christ," said Sean, "that's some logic. See if you were driving along here and you saw the pair of us tramps standing about with our thumbs out, would you stop for us?"

"Ay, I would," said Billy. He meant it.

"Well, you'd be fucking daft," said Sean.

"Well, who would you stop for, if you were driving along?"

"Michelle Pfeiffer," said Sean without hesitation. "I'd stop for her."

"Ay, well your logic's as shite as mine. What's Michelle Pfeiffer doing hitching lifts in Scotland in the pouring rain?"

"How do I fucking ken? It might be in a picture or something. She does real things in the fucking pictures."

After a pause, Sean started up again.

"All right, no Michelle Pfeiffer. Any bird. I'd stop for any bird."

"Supposing she had a bloke with her?"

"Well, of course I fucking wouldna. I'm only picking her up to fucking shag her, amn't I?"

Sean tried to roll a fag. As fast as he worked the paper got soaked and torn. On the third attempt he dropped the tobacco pack on the road and then the rest of the papers. He saved the tobacco but the papers were ruined. "Bastarting fucking rain!" he shouted, kicking the papers across the road.

Billy thought, how do I know about Jonahs? We must have done it at Sunday school or something. Christ, *that* was a long time ago! Funny to think his folks had been quite religious in those days, wanted him to know his Bible and that. A Jonah was someone who slept soundly on the lower deck while the storm raged and worried sailors jettisoned cargo. He looked at Sean and then he looked at himself. Maybe I've got this wrong, he thought.

"Maybe we should split up," he heard himself say.

"What?" said Sean.

"I'm just thinking, if we split up there's mair chance of us getting lifts out of here if anybody does stop. Further up the road too. I mean, if we're going to get to Kenny in time."

Sean looked at him. "You want us to split up?" he said.

"I'm just thinking there'd be more chance, maybe. . . ."

Sean gobbed on the road again, then he said, "It's me, isn't it? You don't think we're going to get there the pair of us, do you?"

"Well, we shouldn't have ever come this way in the first place."

"Ay, you wouldn't be blaming me if you'd got your fucking hole, would ye?"

"Ay, but I didn't, did I? In fact, we never even found the women, Sean. All I'm saying is, it's taken us all day to get from that hotel to this wee village, one lift, and we're probably cutting our chances in half sticking thegither."

"There's only been three cars in the last hour and they were all full. The road's no exactly been teeming with cars going, sorry lads, only room for one of yous, has it?"

"It's just with the rucksacks and everything. If we'd gone up the A9 on our own we'd be there by now."

"You should have thought about that when we set out. It's no my fucking fault there's no traffic on the road. Think I'm bad for you or something?"

"Naw. But we've no been having much luck the last day or two, have we?"

"Oh, that's my fault, is it? Think I'm bad luck, ya bastard? Well, I'll tell you, you're no Mr Opportunity fucking Knocks yourself."

"All right," said Billy. "All right, all right, all right! I'm just getting depressed, that's all."

"Join the club," said Sean. They stood listening to the rain falling and the total absence of traffic.

"I mean," said Billy, "I'm no even sure about this job either."

Sean came over to him and stood with his face at an angle an inch or two away from Billy's. "Say that again?" he said.

Billy shrugged. The movement caused more rain to trickle down his back. This bothered him more than Sean's aggression, which was all thunder and no lightning anyway.

"Are you saying the job's no definite?" Sean wanted to know.

"Naw," said Billy, "course it is. If we get there in time. That's no what I mean. I mean, the ethics of it."

"Aw, no that again," said Sean. "I thought we'd been through all that."

"Ay, we have," said Billy, "but I'm still turning it over. It's no that simple."

"It's this bloody simple," said Sean. "If we don't do the work some other cunt will. That's all there is to it."

He stamped his feet up and down the road to get the circulation going. After a couple of minutes he stopped.

"Bugger this," he said. "I'm freezing to death here. I'm away back for another pot of tea off that nice wee lassie."

"May as well stick it out now we're soaked," said Billy. "Somebody's got to come by sooner or later."

"Ay, probably later. Come on, let's go back and get warmed up."

"Ay, maybe." Billy pulled back his jacket sleeve to check his watch. "Look, it's just gone quarter past four. Give it till half-past and if we're still here we'll go back."

"Christ, the cafe'll probably close at half-four. Nothing's coming, Billy. Let's go for the tea."

"We've got to get out of here, Sean. There's a guy coming up the road this minute that's destined to stop for us. No, I'm wrong, it's no a guy, it's this gorgeous oversexed American divorcee on her holidays, looking for some local talent. And her pal. I don't want to miss the only lift going just for another cup of tea."

"Well, I'm chancing it. We'll take it in shifts. Heads I go first, tails you stay, ha ha. Then when I come back you can go. Come and get us if anyone stops, eh?"

"Come on, Sean, you can't get folk to stop and then say, oh, eh, by the way, could you just back up the road to that wee tea-shop there, my mate's just finishing his scones. I mean, can you?"

"Well, I'm fucking away. You coming or staying?"

"I'm staying. I'll wait till half-past."

Neither of them would give way. Sean walked off a few yards. Billy tried to put some action into standing his ground. This was the deal, if it was one: Billy would make his point of principle for fifteen minutes, then join Sean in the cafe. He would make his stand and hope a car wouldn't come along to put it to the test. Sean slouched off through the rain towards the cafe.

The ethics of it. The night before, waiting for the women, they'd had this long discussion about the tree-felling. It was a programme Billy had seen on the telly that started him off, about this massive Forestry Commission plantation that had been sold off to some pop-group or Terry Wogan or someone. It had been planted in the 1950s, according to a plan. The plan was that the trees would be regenerative, if that was the word. You'd harvest them over a period of thirty years or so, so that the next lot would have grown up by the time you'd finished. The crofters in the area could get part-time work every single year for decades, taking out the mature trees in partnership with the Commission. The whole thing was about community involvement.

"Then the Forestry Commission's forced to sell it off when the trees are about to mature and some rich bastard buys it who never comes near the place and one day his accountant tells him to realise his assets and take the whole fucking lot out. That doesna seem right at all to me."

"Aw, come on," said Sean, "don't get so pious. You're in it just the same as everyone. You need the work and I need the work, and what's more we can do the work. If it wasn't us it would be someone else."

"That's the point, though. It shouldn't be us. It should be about sustaining the local population, not bringing in the flying squads."

"The world's fucking changed, Billy," said Sean. "You might not like it much, and I might not like it, but it's changed and you have to change with it. See when they sold off British Telecom and British Gas and that? Did you buy the shares and make a few hundred quid selling them on?"

"No," said Billy. "That wasna right either. How, did you?"

"No, but no out of principle. I didna have any cash or I would have done. And there was plenty of folk I ken that did."

"Ay, and what have they got to show for it now? They might have made a few bob but look at how much profit B.T. makes these days. Hundreds of pounds every bloody second. And how much of that are you and me and anybody else in Hicksville Scotland ever going to see? Not a fucking penny."

"Well, moaning about the rights and wrongs of it isn't going to make it better. You had your chance for a slice of the action and you missed it."

"We both did," said Billy. This forestry thing, it was like American mining companies ripping off Indian land for uranium or something. The same idea. Sean shrugged. "Grab it when you see it," he said. "Work, women, money. That's the only way to live these days."

Billy and Sean. It sounded like a sectarian stand-up comedy act, and in a way that was exactly what they were. They got on all right, they played off against each other, but Billy wouldn't have said they'd ever got close. He wouldn't say that about him and anybody though. Especially not his male friends. You just didn't do it. The closest you got was kicking a ball about, or on the terracing watching Scotland (at club level it was different teams, of course, for him and Sean), or drunk together in the pub. You needed something external like that to be able to show your affection, any warmth. So probably the closeness wasn't even there if you took away the circumstances. It was all artificially induced. Men were like herds of rutting stags, or tigers wandering about in the jungle. They didn't much like each other's company so they invented sport and pubs to make it bearable. What they really wanted to do was roam around on their own, occasionally home in on unsuspecting women and engage in an elaborate mating ceremony, then fuck off into the jungle again. Or up on the moors or wherever.

Women now, that was different. Women friends were close to each other. Christ, they wore each other's clothes and shared their beds and their most intimate secrets and suchlike. He couldn't imagine what that must be like. It must be great but frightening too. Making yourself so vulnerable. But warm too, when it was working right. And of course a man and a woman could be like that. The man could get a real friend out of his female lover. What did the woman get? She might get a lover out of a male friend but could she get a friend out of her lover? Not according to the accepted wisdom, it seemed.

Women friends. He had a few. There was Marian that worked behind the bar at his local, but she was every man's friend. You could talk to Marian about whatever you wanted and she'd listen but that was her job, somehow even though you could have a great crack with her you felt she wouldn't let you get close to her, she had another life when she came round the bar. Good for her too, you didn't grudge her that. He was still friendly with a couple of old girlfriends. They were married now, to mates of his, and that was fine, there was no aggro about it, and he could chat to them and dance with them at parties and nobody cared. But there was a line there, a line beyond which the conversation could not go. Partly the line was drawn by himself, but mostly it was there because of conventions. You do not discuss your sexual frustrations with your mate's wife who happens to be an old flame, for example. Just not the done thing, open to misinterpretation *et cetera* by all parties concerned. Sometimes—at nights out or weddings, say, especially weddings—he saw the women in wee groups, talking nineteen to the dozen, and even though physically there was no barrier in fact he knew they were on the far side of the line. He'd look across the dance-floor and all he'd see was drunk men standing at the bar together, and single men circling the dancers.

He was sick of the male thing. If he could do it for another couple of years maybe he could stop, get into his secure place, and start being human. That's what he felt like, that most of his life he spent not being human, not being himself, but trying to play a role. He looked at a guy like Sean and he thought maybe he should just give in, but it wasn't good enough. That was his trouble. Nothing was good enough for him. He couldn't help thinking beyond where he was.

Jonah in the Bible. Some folks called him Jonas, was that right? He seemed to remember that from somewhere. Anyway, whatever his name was, the thing about him was if he hadn't run away from God he'd have been all right. It was because he was running away from God that he was jinxed. When the storm blew up the crew knew that meant someone was bad luck, so they drew lots to find out who, and it was Jonah. So they threw him overboard and he got swallowed by the whale. But suppose it hadn't been him? Suppose it was someone else that was jinxed? He drew the short straw but that wasn't exactly conclusive evidence. Then he came up with this shite about having displeased God, so they took that as proof and chucked him in the sea. He was Jewish and they weren't, that was another thing. This business of upsetting his God wouldn't mean much to them, it wouldn't be a proper reason for pinning the blame on him, and anyway he'd told them about it before the storm. What if they'd got rid of him and the storm hadn't died down, would they have drawn lots again, thrown each other in until it stopped? No, that would have made the whole story pointless. The point was, the only thing that made Jonah the Jonah was the story. It had to be him for the story to work.

There was a swishing sound and a car came into view out of the village, its headlights taking Billy by surprise. However his thumb was experienced, it went out instantly, and as if it exerted some magical influence the car slowed to a halt beside him. Great moments, thought Billy. He still got a thrill when it happened. He stepped over just as the driver was leaning across to open the passenger door.

"How far you going, pal?"

"Inverness," said the driver. A man in shirt-sleeves and tie. His jacket was hung on a plastic peg behind him. "That any use to you?"

"Ay, brilliant," said Billy. "Eh, I've got a rucksack here, is that all right?"

"Ay," said the driver. "Just sling it in the boot, there's plenty room." He pressed or pulled some control under the dashboard and the boot sprang open.

"Great," said Billy. He looked back down the road for Sean, then at his watch. It was ten to five. Come on, ya bastard, where are you, stuck in the cludgie or something? He tried to take his time loading the rucksack into the boot and closing it.

"That you first in the queue, son?" the driver called. Billy went back to the open door. "What's that?" he said.

"I'm saying, are you in a queue? I see there's another rucksack there."

"Ay, well, actually," said Billy, pointing back to the village. "Eh, it's just like, there's someone else."

"I can see that. Well, come on, hop in, the seat's getting wet."

"Ay, I mean, it's my mate like. He's back there at the cafe."

The driver leaned right over again, his face staring up into

Billy's. He was some kind of sales rep, probably. He looked quite a hardman.

"Right, well, I haven't got all day. I'm doing you a favour, son. Are you coming or not?"

Billy hesitated again, his hand on the passenger door. There was still no sign of Sean. He'd be chatting up that lassie behind the counter, he knew it, he could just about hear him at it.

The driver revved his engine. "Fuck's sake," he said. "You didn't have your thumb out in the fucking rain for nothing, did ye? Make up your mind, pal."

"Sorry," said Billy. From Inverness he could go anywhere. It wasn't the kind of statement you ever expected to hear—"From Inverness you can go anywhere!"—but it was true. Maybe he'd keep going north, find Kenny, get the job. Or maybe he'd tell him, no, I can't do it, Kenny, I can't take part in this massacre, and head off back down the A9. Or just not bother. Aberdeen, maybe. Try to get out on the rigs again. Aberdeen, then Australia. Ay, and maybe it was him after all, he'd get thrown overboard, swallowed by a big fish.

This was all in a moment. A moment like all these moments in his life when he felt he was being tossed like a coin. For a moment the chances hang spinning in the air, and then you call.

"Right," he said to the driver above the noise of the rain. He almost shouted it.

The Claw

My grandfather's hand is turning into a claw. That's what I'm thinking as I watch it raise the coffee cup. The finger-joints are swollen and the fingers themselves permanently curled, and the tone of the flesh is distorted by bruise-like browns and blues. Liver-spots, I think the term is. They come with old age. The grip on my arm when he pulled up out of his chair to greet me was so fierce that it felt like he would never let go. Looking at the hand now, hard and unyielding on the fussy handle of the cup, it seems independent of the rest of him. Evidently the brain is still sending out orders, but between it and the claw everything else is crumbling.

His upper arms are thin as ropes, his whole structure like some skeletal macramé. He can barely walk across the room even with his sticks or a zimmer. He needs help to get to the bathroom or to the dining-room. The latter journey is painfully slow, involving him being loaded into the chairlift at the top of the staircase and helped out of it at the bottom. When the staff are too busy they bring the meals to his room instead. This is happening more and more, I know, because he tells me. "They're keeping me a prisoner here," he says loudly, before the woman who brought the tray has closed the door behind her. I laugh in a way that is supposed to sound to her like an apology.

In addition to the infirmity of his legs, other faults have developed in the last year. He likens himself to a motor car— that's what he calls it—and says that with 98,000 miles on the clock it's not surprising that the bodywork is a bit rusty and some things don't work very well any more. He's already had two hip replacement operations and now he says they're not making the parts for his model, so he won't be going up on the ramp again, thank you very much.

Or to put it another way: he says he's on borrowed time, each year he chalks up beyond the biblical span a debt that God might call in at any moment. He can no longer go to church, of course. The Minister comes every so often, and twice a year he receives his own private communion. His faith is unquestionable, but what exactly it is has never been discussed. He would resent even the Minister—especially the Minister—interfering in that matter.

His bladder is weak, his bowel easily upset. He can no longer take a bath without assistance. He is almost totally blind and even with his hearing-aid turned up full he is pretty deaf— although everybody says he sees and hears more than he lets on. I find this idea disconcerting, as his knowledge of me is constructed on a set of evasions and unrevealed truths and I wonder if he can hear them in my voice or see them in my smile. When someone has lost the full use of their senses you become careless and drop your guard. But if my grandfather has his suspicions he does not display them. That is not the done thing with him. He'll wait to be told, and if he's told nothing he'll assume there's a conspiracy and come up with his own theory to fit it.

He has a very ordered mind, which has always extended to his own presentation. He shaves every morning with an electric shaver and takes a pride in always wearing a collar and tie, and having clean shoes. Not that the shoes can get dirty as he never leaves the home now, not for birthdays or weddings or Christmas or any other family occasion. "There's only one event I can think of that I'll get out of here for," he says. "I hope you'll all attend!" He has three children, eight grandchildren and twelve great-grandchildren and on each of their birthdays a card drops through the letter-box, the envelope addressed in an anonymous hand, his signature scrawled under the greeting. This year he sent mine to my mother as I was in America again, and she forwarded it to me. Various multi-coloured cats in acrobatic poses spelt out the words HAPPY BIRTHDAY. It was months ago but one of the first things he said to me when I got back was, "Did you get my card? I sent it to your mother. One of the people here chose it for me. They said it had a lot of cats on it. I hope you don't dislike cats very much." It takes someone born in

47

another century to come out with a sentence like that.

The woman who brought the coffee—"one of the people here"—her name is Meg. She called him "Mr Stewart", and smiled at me one of those understanding smiles that go with the job. Most of the residents get called by their first names, but not my grandfather. It is not so much that he is too formidable, rather that there is a sense of propriety about him which defies over-familiarity. Probably this becomes more important as, bit by bit, his physical dignity is stripped away. A decade separates him from nearly all the other residents, a generation or two from the staff, and from me.

I watch the claw move over the table between us, locating the saucer, then the plate with the biscuits, then one of the pink wafers. Even at such a late stage the brain can still learn new tricks: in this case, how to be blind. Three times I have visited him since I came back, three times in three months, and each time his body is frailer but his face seems stronger, in spite of the sightless eyes. It's as though the mind has finally lost patience with the useless flesh which encumbers it. My grandfather is ninety-eight. He had a turn last year and everybody thought he was on the way out but now his mind has rallied and, although he doesn't mention it, he must be aiming for the hundred and that fabled telegram. There were times when people of his vintage feared the arrival of official telegrams, but now the only one he is going to get is a hope and a challenge, growing nearer with each passing day.

I am only thirty-five but watching him I feel as old as he looks. I am HIV-positive. In the last year I've studied my soul from all sides, and every morning I begin the examination again.

"New York," he says. He says it as if the novelty has not worn off the name, as if English York should still feel aggrieved at being usurped. "It must be very exciting. Of course I've never been to any of these places." I'm not fooled by the self-effacement—we're all well used to the implications by now: I've never lived, I've never done anything except this—this getting to be an old man; you young people today live lives we could never have imagined. This from a man who spent six months being shelled on a beach at Gallipoli, then a year in the mud in France, watching the other young men around him dying, and wondering if the war would be over before his turn came.

I went from extreme youth to some kind of wisdom in less than ten years. Maybe a war does that for you too, I wouldn't know. I have to say that we—I mean our community in New York—reacted very quickly once we realised the horror that was upon us. But the damage was already done: we had been too much of a community and we suffered like one of those companies wiped out on the Somme, when all the men came from one town or district. God dispensing justice, some say.

"I've never really known any Americans," he tells me. "Never had much dealings with them. Of course a lot of our people ended up there." By this he means the emigrants: our people became their people. "A big country," he says, "with great cities. I should like to have seen some of those cities. A lot of opportunity there, I should imagine."

I have known many Americans, and I have taken opportunities and had experiences in their greatest city which if I were to tell him would appal my grandfather, assuming that he believed his own flesh and blood capable of such things. If I were to tell him, but naturally I will not. My years over there, as far as he knows, have been about study and travel and more study, and a little bar and restaurant work on the side to help finance me, and that famous American hospitality. But in reality it was the friends who kept me there, kept me going back. Yes, I have known many Americans, and they have known me. This was in the days of manifest destiny, when we still believed opportunity was there for the taking. Of course we were hated and feared for it. We always have been.

I don't know if I will be going back. I'm not even sure if they would let me through immigration.

"A lot of Irish there too," says my grandfather. "The Scots and the Irish have plenty in common in their history." He says this with wonder in his voice, as though it has just occurred to him, although it's a familiar preamble. It is one of the things that amazes me about him: his constant ability to re-energise old

49

facts and thoughts that have been his companions longer now than any living thing on earth. He never tires of them. Now that I have lost so many, my lovers and other friends, I understand this honing of memory. What was once tedious to me I see has a kind of comfort. I find myself welcoming what comes next: his recital of the league table of national prejudice.

"Always liked the Irish—friendly, open people. Take life as they find it. Tragic as well, of course, their history—like ours—more so. Don't like the Welsh—never trusted them. The English, well, we all have to get on with the English, don't we? Spent most of my working life among them. London. Hm, yes, they were always very civil, I have to say. They liked us, you know, when we went to London. We were thorough, exact. What's the word? Conscientious. Yes, we were conscientious."

He pauses. He has dealt with these islands. His mind drifts across the sea.

"I like the French." He decides in their favour, as he always does. In the twenties it was a little risqué to like the French, and now it always will be. "Delightful people. And the Italians—charming. Never could run anything though, not even under Mussolini." The Italians are forgiven their little mistake; it wasn't really anything they could *help*. As usual, the fun dries up here. Naturally no one of his generation need even consider the possibility of liking the Germans. And the Germans are about as far as one seriously needs to go in such a line of thought. All those conflicts in the Middle East, all those shades of nation and race—Asia, Africa, the Americas—too distant, too *different*. And yet once he said to me, shaking his head at some new conflagration, "We must, we must try to understand. Otherwise it'll just go on and on as it always has."

There it is. My grandfather is like the rest of us, caught between history and hope, but history weighs heavy in his scales now, and every year it feeds faster and faster, gobbling up hope. He looks back on his life and it isn't just that he's had the best years of it, it's that it's over, actually over, and all he can do is sit in his armchair which faces the spot where the portable TV used to be and wait for a telegram and whatever it is his faith has promised him.

Anyway, it's nonsense to say he has not lived! Quite apart from the war. He worked in London for nearly four decades as an accountant, maybe not the most glamorous of professions but—what decades! The twenties, thirties, forties and fifties! In the twenties, when the civil war was on, he went to Dublin every year to oversee an audit for a client company there. He used to play golf with the company chairman. "You'll be fine with me, don't you worry," the chairman would assure him—a Brit in the new, bloodily born Free State. On the ninth tee the chairman pointed to a dyke running alongside the course and said to him: "Just last week I was playing here, there was a foursome up ahead on the fairway, these three fellows with guns came out of nowhere, took one of the foursome away and shot him against the wall. I tell you, it shakes you up, a thing like that. We didn't know whether we should finish our round or not." That's the Irish for you, says my grandfather. He chuckles at the memory.

When he had his turn last year his memory went into overdrive. My mother had it partly from himself, partly from the staff. They would find him at night in his pyjamas in the corridor, fuelled by something so powerful that it made him able to walk completely unaided. It was a struggle to persuade him back to bed. Once he was looking for his wife. Once he said he was trying not to step on the faces of the dead men on the floor. Perhaps this is how we prepare for death, by revisiting the people that were dearest to us, or whose being taken from us was the worst to bear. Perhaps we have to apologise for surviving.

I'm not ready to do that yet. My people are not far enough away.

My grandfather grew up in and around Dundee. As the century turned he was five, then six. One day his father, who was a lawyer and well-connected, took him on an expedition with a friend who had just bought a motor car. They drove all the way to Perth and made a telephone call to say they had arrived safely. Then they had tea at the Station Hotel before setting out on the return journey. My grandfather reckons he must have been one of the first people to make that trip by car. I consider this to be a miraculous story; so simple, so innocent. I always encourage him to tell it.

"Of course, nowadays people fly all over the world and don't think anything of it!" he says. "Like you. You've been to all sorts of places, done all sorts of things."

How can I tell him, how could he believe me, that I long to be that little boy, ecstatic on that dusty road beside the Tay? How can I tell him that I think I know what lies between that happy, excited trust in the transport of the future and the tough old bird who sits opposite me now, his claw neatly placing the wafer biscuit on the saucer? How can I tell him that I would willingly travel back and forth on that road for eternity, and never tire of it? I would like to try to explain, to say that I've been in the trenches too, that I have held the heads of my dying friends and that the wound I have carried home with me has not bought me safety. He's so incredibly old. Nothing should surprise him any more.

Instead we sit and talk about jobs I might do, places I might go next. I'll say this for him, he has never criticised my lack of career. There is envy in there of course. He never had the chance. But then again, he believes life is for the taking. "Take it!" he says. "You've nothing to lose."

Then something goes wrong. He puts his cup and saucer down too suddenly, and a little spurt of coffee and pink wafer shoots out over his chin and stains his tie. His face seems to collapse and drain of colour. He hunches forward. "I don't feel well," he says. The words are small and childlike.

There is a bell which I press for help, and while we're waiting I reach out and take his hard hand in mine. "It's all right, someone'll be here in a moment." The trouble is, in spite of everything, I'm still useless in these situations. I don't know what to say or do, except to touch. The door opens and it's Meg who enters. "Now, Mr Stewart, are you not feeling well?" "He seemed fine," I tell her, "and then everything suddenly seemed to stop." "It sometimes happens," she says, "it sometimes happens. He just needs to lie down for a while. He gets terribly tired, you see."

Between us we help him over to the bed. He keeps saying he is very sorry to cause a fuss. Meg quiets him, gently lays him on the bed. Suddenly I see the fear swirling in his milky eyes. "Who's that, who's that?" "It's only me," she says . "It's Meg." I feel helpless and afraid too, and draw back a little. Too many things are flooding in. Meg sits beside him on the bed, stroking his hand. This is a country where it still falls to the women to save us. To bear us, to tend us, to take our hands, to comfort us even to the grave. "Will he be okay?" I ask. She holds me with a look—there is kindness in it, I think, and maybe scorn too, it's hard to tell—as if she can see me exactly as my grandfather cannot, as if she knows what's going on in my heart. Maybe she'll gossip over her tea downstairs: "That grandson of his, he's a bit, you know. . . . Doesn't look too well himself either." The kind of things my own mother can't admit. Meg looks about ages with her. She's probably got a son too, in the army or something.

Then she smiles at me and says, "Don't worry, it's just sleep, he just needs to sleep. It'll be all right."

"I'd better go," I say. "Yes," she says, "I think so. And don't worry." No scorn, then, just kindness. I think I'd rather have the scorn. "Goodbye," I say to him, but of course he doesn't hear. I touch his hand, but he probably thinks it's Meg, if he notices at all. Suddenly I wish I was away, and never coming back. I can't stand the thought of invalids. Of being at the mercy of others.

Squibs

The Edinburgh Summit

It was the proudest day of my life when Big Norrie asked me to be on the Scottish delegation to the Edinburgh Euro Summit.

We booked into Mrs Fankle's guesthouse early so we'd have time to write the postcards. None of your flash city centre hotels for us, oh no, we wanted to demonstrate our sense of fiscal responsibility. The guesthouse was called Taigh na Noatinit. "One bathroom for all and all for one," said Neil, showing solidarity.

"Any house rules, Mrs F.?" called Norrie from in front of the fire. "Just so we know where we stand."

"No standing in front of the fire," said Mrs Fankle firmly. "It's there for show, not so's the likes of you can toast your fat arse. And no visitors in rooms after 1979."

That seemed to knock auld Geordie's plans for an all-night session on the head. Still, as Norrie said, we weren't here for pleasure. Always been a bit of a hardline Calvinist, has Norrie. Many's the time he's said to me after I've made a wee pun or some other form of wordplay, "Mind now, young fellow, we're not here for pleasure."

We had our speeches all worked out. Norrie was to welcome the other delegates and extend an invitation to the ceilidh that evening. Neil was going to demand a bigger fish rebate for Scotland. I was putting the finishing touches to my epic poem, *To Circumvent the Bus Fare*, or *Alva Reborn*. Geordie thought he'd just play some tunes on his tin whistle and try to raise a few bob from the tourists.

Neil was a bit worried about the lack of women in our group. After all we wanted to represent the new enlightened face of our country. We took a vote on it and by an overwhelming majority it was agreed we'd ask Mrs Fankle if she'd like to come. However she told us—a bit sharpish, I thought—that she had wolves to feed and mouths to keep from the door and no time for our nonsense. Just shows you, said Norrie, once we were out of earshot, you try to do them a favour and they bite your lug off.

We arrived at the Palais in good style on a Number 2, though unfortunately a ticket inspector got on and we had to pay up. Heads held high we marched up to the gate. Would you credit it? The polis on the gate wouldn't let us in. He said we didn't have passes. "For heaven's sake, laddie," said Norrie, "we're the host delegation. This is our capital city, we don't need passes." At this juncture the polis pointed out several figures in black on the battlements who had their rifles trained on us. "Get lost before I start taking you seriously," he said.

We were a bit deflated, to say the least. But Geordie soon cheered us up. He said he thought he knew some of the Danes—he'd met them at the football in the summer. We could come back at dinner-time and try and sneak in on one of their passes.

In the meantime it was too cold to stand around, so we went over to the Meadows for a kickabout—Norrie always carries a ball with him, just in case. "You never know when it'll come in handy," he told me once. How right he was! We had a good bit of exercise, and the fresh air was a tonic. But then a bloke in a grey raincoat came along and spoiled our fun. Whenever our backs were turned he kept moving the goalposts, which consisted of Norrie's sweatshirt and my epic poem.

I went over to reason with him. He was a dull-looking man in glasses.

"Look," I said, "this is our game, just leave us alone will you?"

"I'm not interfering," he said flatly, "I'm just taking stock."

I went back to Norrie and told him what he'd said. Norrie looked him over. "I'll tell you who he is," he said. "He's a talent scout. Come on, lads, throw yourselves about, impress the guy. He's probably from one of the big Italian clubs, looking for fresh blood."

But after a while the man wandered off towards the swings. Norrie shouted after him, "Hey Mister, don't go. We're only part of a whole team. We're brilliant. Stay and watch us."

But he didn't seem to hear.

"What'll we call ourselves, Norrie?" I asked. It was exciting to be in on something new and exciting.

Norrie's face was set in concentration.

"I know, I know," said wee Neil, jumping up and down. "How about Scotland Albion?"

The trouble with Neil is he's got no imagination.

Sir Walter's Nightmare

Sophia and Anne, clinging to each other in terror, cowered behind the thick drapes of the drawing-room curtains. They dared not open them even a fraction, for fear that the chink of light might reveal their presence to the mob. Yet in truth they did not need to peer out. The wild shrieks, the crash of breaking glass and the smell of burning which assailed their senses told only too well of the destruction in progress in the streets outside.

"Oh, would that John were here!" cried Anne tearfully. Sophia, who, in Lockhart's absence, was conscious of a responsibility for her sister which might not otherwise have checked her own rising emotions, reasoned with her as calmly as the circumstances allowed.

"Fear not, dearest one," she urged. "Surely there are prudent and honourable leaders among the multitude, who, as they have engaged in that cause through a sense of injustice, however inflamed by the passions aroused by the intemperate and hasty actions of desperate men, will never allow the baser instincts of their fellows to perpetrate an unlawful act of violence against innocent and defenceless creatures such as ourselves."

"But we are not innocent!" wept Anne, who, as well as being the younger, was perhaps the weaker of the two. "For years the interest to which we adhere has stubbornly denied the basic right of democracy to the Scottish people. Oh, Sophia, I know how much father detests the very thought of democracy, and I understand how genuine is John's belief that the people do not know what is best for them, but surely, when the pressure for change is so overwhelmingly apparent, such a tiny minority, howsoever honest their motives may be, cannot stand in the way for ever!"

"Yes, dear sister," said Sophia, "I do share with you the belief that had it only been possible to persuade father's political friends to give gracefully what was once demanded peaceably and without threat of violence, this present crisis might have been avoided. Rather than this,"—and with a wave of her hand she indicated the world outside their little sanctuary—"it would indeed have been better to sink to a subordinate species of Northumberland, but it appears that the general populace think otherwise. Oh, Anne, the ways of politics are strange, and not for feminine minds to question!" Here she broke off, for a renewed chorus of angry voices sounded, as it seemed, directly outside the window. As the full import of the rioters' demands reached them, Anne sank insensible in the other's arms, while even Sophia's steadfast and courageous resolve was shaken by the dreadful words that carried on the wind:—
"Save our regiments! Save our regiments! Save our regiments!"

The Old Pretender

I was sitting on the bus next to an unshaven, shabbily dressed man holding a plastic bucket on his lap. I'd been trying to read the paper but I gave up as the motion of the bus was making me feel sick. Also, my neighbour kept clearing his throat in a particularly noisy and disgusting manner and ejecting the mucous accumulation into his bucket. After the third or fourth time I looked around for somewhere else to sit but the bus was full.

"I say, must you do that in public?" I asked him.

"Fuck off," he said.

"I beg your pardon?" I said but he interrupted me—"Sorry, son, ye'll need tae speak up, I'm a wee bit corned beef, ken."

Perhaps I had misheard him. I gave him the benefit of the doubt.

"Couldn't you do that somewhere else?" I asked.

"Eh? Well, I could dae it on the flair I suppose but I'd be pit aff the bus. Naw, the bucket's the best place for it, nae question."

I counted to five. "What is wrong with you?" I inquired.

"I'm juist efter tellin ye, son, I'm a bit deif. Comes o staunin next tae a forty-eight pounder for three days and nights while it wis batterin the hell out o the Hun."

There was another volley of rasping and the rattle of gunk on the sides of the bucket.

I looked him up and down suspiciously. In spite of his rough beard and generally unkempt appearance, I doubted he was more than a few years older than myself.

"Are you telling me that you fought in the war?"

"Ay, I did that, two year on the Western Front. I saw men die in thousans, dug fifty miles o trenches, ate rats for tea mair than once, and wis gassed three times and survived. That's whit did for ma lungs," he added, expectorating still more of the contents of his innards as if to prove the point.

"Ah," I said, now firmly convinced that I was sitting next to a madman, "I misunderstood you. I thought you meant the *Second* World War."

"The whit?" he said. "Naw, the Great War, the Great War. Funny that, it wisna that fuckin great at all. Mind you, I met some fine lads out there." His eyes glazed over with what presumably were fond memories. "Auld sodgers niver die," he said. "Wee Tammy McCutcheon, Sandy MacPhail, Andy Dunlop. That wis some team. Oh, and Sergeant Erskine, whit a holy terror *he* wis! Uised tae send aa thae poufter poets ower the tap first. 'On ye go, ya jessies,' he'd shout as the German shells rained doun, 'bet ye canna think o somethin tae rhyme wi that bluidy racket!'"

The reminiscence set off another bout of hacking. What sounded like a regiment of tackety boots scraped past the barbed wire of his throat and a few more shovelfuls of Passchendaele mud spattered into the bucket.

"You were never in the First World War," I said derisively. "You're not even old enough to have fought in Malaya."

"Your whit?" Then he charged on, ignoring me totally. "Ay, but whit for, whit for? Little Belgium, hames fit for heroes, the British bluidy Empire. I tell ye, the warkin man wis duped, duped guid and proper." The bus suddenly lurched and there was a screeching of brakes and the blaring of horns. "Naw! Naw!" he screamed. "I canna staun it!" My right ear was ringing. "Shell shock," he said without apology. "I'm a broken man, so I am." He shook the bucket and I heard a horrible slorping sound.

I was about to get up as my stop was only a few minutes away, when another voice croaked at my back. "Would you let me go first, please?" I half-turned and this time it was a very old white-haired man with a walking-stick and a lovely lilting voice. "Sorry," he said, "it takes me all my time to get from one end of the bus to the other."

I let him go past and stood up after him. "Of course," I said. "Here, let me give you a hand."

"Fuckin wee upstart." Behind me the words echoed in the bucket. "Get yersel a haircut."

The old gent and I made it to the front of the bus. We both wanted the same stop. I helped him onto the grass verge and together we watched the bus pull away into the distance. We were out in the country now, just the two of us, miles from anywhere.

"Thank you so much," he said. He was one of the old school. "I'm not as quick as I was when I was your age. It's my gammy leg, you know. Musket ball, Prestonpans, '45."

Poetic Injustice

The shop window stopped me in its tracks. I was already depressed with everything but this was too much.

Or rather, it wasn't the window itself that shocked me, for it

59

was a nondescript and unimpressive frontage, but its contents. It was full of row upon row of wee plastic figures in bright red kilts, each clutching a pipe and with a great mass of hair pouring backwards from the brow. There must have been fifty at least of the things, and in their midst a handwritten sign proclaimed:

MACDIARMIGONKS—ONLY 40p EACH
(3 for a pound)

The door jingled as I stepped inside. I was outraged. "MacDiarmigonks!" I spluttered at the man behind the counter. "What's the meaning of it?"

He was small and bald and had a pencil behind his right ear. In his brown coat and round glasses he was like a shopkeeper from a previous age. Would he add up your purchases on the side of a paper bag before ringing the total through the till?

He said nothing in answer to my question, but merely made a vague, hopeless gesture around the shelves. It was astonishing. There were even more of the nasty creatures inside. I picked one up and saw printed on the base the legend "Made In" but I couldn't bear to read any further. I didn't know which word would be more offensive. There were also plaster of Paris statuettes of another kilty with flaming orange hair and an empty whisky bottle contemplating a bloody great hairy thistle. There were tee-shirts hanging up that said, "I was a torpid denizen of the aquarium . . ." on the front, and ". . . until I discovered MacDiarmid" on the back. There were tea-towels that said, "There's a moose loose aboot this hauf-way hoose" and green car-windscreen strips that said, "I amna fou sae muckle as tired, officer!" There were tumblers that said, "The Glass of Pure Water ho-ho" and even covers for toilet seats that said, "Whaur extremes meet". The whole scene was a disgrace to the community.

"Where did all this come from?" I demanded.

"Ah," he began, and it was as if I had uncorked a bottle lying on its side, "the worst mistake of my life. I don't mind telling you that. This fellow comes in one day with his business cards and his big braying voice, says he has a grant from MacEnterprise and he's going to put MacDiarmid firmly on the map. Those were his very words. 'I'm going to do for MacDiarmid what shortbread's done for Burns,' he said. Well, I fell for it. I was hooked and to this day I don't know how. I must have been mad or drunk or hung over or all three. Trade was bad, and when he came in I thought I saw a glimmer of light at the end of the tunnel. Now look at me. I'm drowning in a sea of MacDiarmid kitsch. And the worst thing is, I've driven away all my old customers. All the grannies that bought wee tartan dolls and trays with pictures of Scottie dogs on them—they won't come here any more with that dreadful communist in the window."

"What about the tourists?" I asked. "Or the younger generation?"

"No," he said, shaking his head. "It's hopeless. I might as well lock up the shop and go home." He picked up one of the gonks and ruefully ran a finger through its hair. "He just hasn't captured the popular imagination," he sighed.

By God he was a miserable wee man. I left his shop then, and as I opened the door a bell rang again. I had been despondent, then stunned, then angry. Now I felt a kind of grim elation. Things weren't so bad after all, I was thinking. I saw a glimmer of light at the end of the tunnel.

Bastards

Across the way, on the corner, Shandon saw the lights of a bar. The streets around here were deserted. He'd been wandering block after block, trying to get his mind round things, round something. Now there was this bar across from him. He felt like he was standing at the edge of one of those lonely-looking downtown American paintings by Edward Hopper, all streetlight and shadow. It was cold, and the bar offered warmth. He crossed over and pushed in through the door.

The place was almost empty, the lights were up and there was no music playing. Probably the lights had never been dimmed, and there was no evidence of a juke-box or any other sound-system. It was ten to eleven.

The man behind the bar was reading a paper. He didn't look like he was expecting a last-minute rush. Shandon thought, if I was the publican I wouldn't bother applying for a late licence for the place, not midweek anyway.

"Still serving?" he asked.

The barman raised his head. "Ay," he said. His tone was mildly indignant, as if he'd been asked to justify his presence.

"A double whisky, then. No, wait a minute, what malts have you got?"

The barman half-turned and pointed to a row of bottles on the gantry. "That's them."

There was nothing very unusual up there. Glenmorangie, Glenfiddich, Glenlivet, Glengoyne. Well, Glengoyne. "A Glengoyne," Shandon said. "A double."

He turned around while the barman measured it out, and took in the other people. A man was sitting further down the bar with a pint, staring into space. In one corner there was a young couple, their glasses empty. They were shrugging on their coats, getting ready to go. In the opposite corner another man and woman, older, maybe in their sixties. What was notable about them was that they were in evening wear. The man had on a black dinner-suit and bow-tie, the woman a blue dress with a stole. Pearls were at her neck and ears. They weren't talking to each other; they were looking over towards him.

"Two pound eighty, please," said the barman. For a moment Shandon was taken aback at the price but then he shrugged and got the money out and pulled the glass towards him. Glengoyne. Lowland. Unpeated. Quite good, he seemed to remember. He made himself wait for it.

If you got twenty-six drams to the bottle and say it cost twenty pound in the shops, but a bar would get it cheaper, say eighteen, that was eighteen divided by twenty-six, which worked out about seventy pence a dram. That was a healthy mark-up, a hundred per cent no less. Jesus. No wonder the place was empty, everybody was drinking at home.

He raised the glass.

Ah, but it was a good one right enough. Glengoyne. He'd forgotten it.

He had to ask himself what he was doing. Had he left her or had he not? And for what, if he had? Physically, of course, he hadn't left her. He'd be going back tonight, of course he would. But had he not left her in every other sense? And how much longer could he not physically leave her, in that case? Jesus.

And what about her, what was she thinking? They never asked each other any more.

He'd gone out halfway through the news, just stood up and said he was going for a walk, maybe a drink, he'd be back later; thinking as he said it that maybe he wouldn't be. She hardly acknowledged his going. On the screen a small country was breaking up; there were bodies everywhere; women and children were herded and huddled together; houses burned; patriots defended what they were doing. He couldn't stand it. But she watched on. What was she thinking?

"What time do you close up at?" he asked.

"Quarter to twelve," said the barman. Shandon was surprised—it hardly seemed worth it. But he knew he'd be staying

63

till the end.

"I'll take a half-pint of heavy," he said. Usually he said please and thank you but not tonight. He wasn't in the mood for it.

"Sixty-five," said the barman. He wasn't wasting his breath either. That was fair enough.

The young couple had left. Only the empty glasses proved that they'd ever been there. The old couple still weren't talking. The man was staring ahead of himself, the woman was fiddling with her necklace. The man down the bar finished his pint and ordered another. Then there was the barman and himself. Christ, they were a right bundle of laughs, the lot of them.

He took his drink in silence. He couldn't think about her. You came out to think about one thing and you ended up thinking about something else. The future. What the hell he was doing with his life, going to do with it. He was angry at himself for being self-indulgent. All over the world folk were simply surviving, or wishing they were dead, one or the other, and he didn't even know what he was doing. What was the point of his life? And why did it go by so fast? And the life that he was leading with her, that she led with him, why did they go on tolerating it? They would have to stop. If they didn't stop it their lives would never have the chance to restart.

He was aware that the man at the far end of the bar had come up beside him, and was addressing his profile:

"I know you. I know who you are."

Shandon thought, Christ, here we go, some fucking eejit, I'm not in the mood to humour some other drunk bastard.

"No you don't," he said, and carried on drinking. Didn't even look at him.

"Ay," said the other man. "Ay, I do." There was something menacing in his voice that made Shandon turn to see if he should recognise him after all. They both eyed each other for a few seconds, and then just as his pinched cheeks and scraggy moustache and slouched shoulders were beginning to look familiar the man said:

"You're the cunt my wife left me for."

64

Shandon felt his skin go cold. It was as if someone had come in the door, letting in a gust of icy air as they did so, but nobody had come in. He wasn't sure how he was going to deal with this, but he really only had the one option—to brazen it out, shut the bastard up before he started.

"Who the fuck do you think you're talking to?"

"I know who I'm talking to. I'm talking to you."

So there was going to be a fight, was that it? Shandon was in no mood for a fight. He wasn't feeling charitable, but he felt too slow, too tired. He wanted the barman to intervene, throw the bastard out, but the barman had disappeared through the back a minute or two before and was on the phone. Probably the guy had seen his chance then, to sneak up on him.

"It's all right," the man said, "relax. I'm not going to batter you. Here, shake on it."

Shandon wasn't daft. He did not extend his hand.

"No," said the guy, "I mean it. No violence." He held one hand up, palm towards him. "My name's Jack Mathieson. Not that you need me to tell you that."

"I don't know you from Adam," said Shandon. "You're making a mistake, and if you don't fuck off you'll be making an even bigger one."

"Nasty," said Mathieson. "That's a nasty streak in you. But I don't want to fight. I want to talk."

"Listen," said Shandon. "Let's get this clear. I don't know you and you don't know me. And I don't want to talk to you. All right?"

"We don't know each other," said Mathieson. "Is that what you're saying?"

"You got it in one, pal," said Shandon.

"Fine," said Mathieson. "If you say so."

"It's not that I say so. It's that it is."

"Fine," said Mathieson. He didn't move.

"Funny," he said. "You look just like the cunt."

By rights Shandon should have let him have it right then and there, but the barman came out again, and not being a witness to the first part of the conversation he would have seen Shandon laying into the smaller, frailer-looking man for no apparent reason. So Shandon moved away slightly, saying to the barman, "Tell this wee shite to get off my back, will you?"

The barman didn't even hesitate. He pointed a finger at Mathieson and nodded down the bar. "On your way, Jack."

Most likely he tried it on with any stranger, any face that might fit. He'd had a disaster of a marriage and never got over it. But it was a bit close for comfort. Maybe Shandon would be like that one day. Ay, maybe he would, if he didn't get his act together and decide what to do with himself. He ordered another whisky—a single—and a pint this time. But coming out to drink on your own was as bad as staying in in front of the wars on the telly. It didn't solve anything. What you needed was something to inspire you.

"I mind, Tom, I mind how I got in with her in the first place. Mind it clear as if it was yesterday."

"Ay." The barman sounded bored, but maybe he thought this way he'd keep the guy down at the end of the bar, away from Shandon.

"Clear as yesterday," said Mathieson.

"How was that then?"

Then Mathieson was talking, as if he had reached a stage of the night or a state of mind which triggered something in him. His voice was calmer than when he'd spoken to Shandon. Shandon stared ahead, not looking; listening.

"She'd just split up with her previous man. I didn't know this at the time but she had. And he was a personal friend, a good friend of mine. Except he ceased to be, after what happened between her and me, I mean. We never spoke to each other again. Probably just as well or he'd have killed me. I met her in this pub somewhere, God I can mind what it looked like, the interior and that, but I'm buggered if I know where it was now. Down in London it was, but where exactly. . . . We were all working down there in these days.

"Anyway, there we were, sitting next to each other in the corner of this pub—I can't even remember but I think she'd

66

phoned me, arranged to meet, and I'd not thought anything of it, and I says to her, where's Paul the night? She says, it's over. Just like that. No tears or nothing. Right in there—it's over.

"And straightaway I'm thinking, you know what I'm thinking, Christ you could be in here mate. You've always fancied her. Could catch her on the rebound if you play your cards right. I mean, I was sorry for her if she was upset, but to be honest that's exactly what I was thinking."

"You weren't wasting any time," said the barman. He was supplying the punctuation, the pauses for drink to be taken.

"Ay, but you know how it is, you caa canny. I waited. I let her do the talking. That was the idea—ease in gently, establish some basic facts. Like, is she angry or distraught or couldn't care less? So I tried it out. I'm sorry, I says. I'm not, she says. Okay, so that meant she was angry.

"Then she says, he could be an animal. Is this in bed, I'm wondering. But no, she goes on, he could be a right bloody animal, farting and belching around my flat like he owned the place."

"Is that what she said?"

"Ay. Well, that made things a wee bit problematic. I'm partial to a wee bit farting and belching myself. All in good time but. Have to break them in slowly sometimes." The barman gave a false kind of laugh, as though he didn't really agree with the sentiment but didn't want to make an issue out of it. "She says, he's a bastard. Well, what a cue. I says, well, it wasn't my place to say anything, but now you're finished I suppose it's all right to say, I never did trust him all together.

"She says, I thought you were his pal. Ay, I says, but if you two are finished like. . . . She says, well, he's a fucking bastard. And she tells me why too. Some of the things. The farting and belching, that was just the tip of the iceberg. What it boiled down to was, he didn't respect her. That's what she reckoned. She kept going on about this respect thing. I couldn't see it myself, but I played along with it. Didn't want to blow my chances, you know. I just sat back and let her use me for an audience, till she got it out of her system. It like, sets you up as the opposite of the guy they're slagging off, know what I mean?

"Anyway, she talks for quite a while, me nodding away in time to her, then she's nothing left to say. So we're sitting there the pair of us, not really drinking much, and I suppose she's thinking over all the things she and him did, all the things that were good while it lasted. Or maybe all the bad things, I don't know . . . the things women think about. Me, I'm wondering, should I put my hand over hers just now, friendly like, comforting, give it a squeeze, or is it too obvious? Too soon? Maybe give it another five minutes and then the arm round her. And then she says, can I trust you, Jack? And I says, course you can, Audrey. And she just kind of snuggles in. That's what she was looking for—reassurance or something. Well, it felt great. I hadn't even put her under any pressure or nothing and she'd just melted.

"Audrey. I always fancied her. And you know, these women, they always go for it. I went home with her that very night. Never spoke to him again, either of us. And then we got married. Five years of it. Makes you think, eh?"

"Ay," said the barman. A sound less like that of someone thinking was hard to imagine.

"She always went for bastards. First him, then me. Then she left me for some other bastard."

"Oh ay?"

Shandon waited for it. He felt himself tensing up. But it was as if Mathieson had forgotten he existed. He downed the rest of his pint. "Oh ay, I'm a bastard all right. No question. We all are. Ay well, it was good while it lasted. I'm away. I'll see you the morra."

"Ay, right you are. Night."

"Night."

And he walked out. Just like that. Never even looked at Shandon again.

Shandon said to the barman, "That guy, does he come in here much?"

"Ay, he's a regular. Was he giving you bother earlier?"

"Ay, nothing serious but. What's his name, do you know?"

"Jack," said the barman. "That's all I know—Jack. You can

get too close to some of these loners."

"An occupational hazard, I would think."

"Ay," said the barman, glancing at him. "Not if I can help it." He went down the bar to get the empty glass. "Are you wanting anything before I close up?"

"Yes, please." It was the old fellow in the dinner-suit. He'd come up behind Shandon without making a sound.

"Same again, Gordon?"

"Same again, Tom, thank you very much." His voice was rich and plummy, not English but what some people would call educated Scots. He had a big chest and thick grey side-whiskers; his silver hair was well combed and oiled. These things seemed to go with the voice: they stood for power, maturity, self-confidence. But when Shandon looked more closely he saw food stains on the white shirt-front, and an unsightly clump of hairs sprouting from his ear.

"All right, my friend?" said the older man. He leaned heavily on the bar, turning sideways to look directly into Shandon's face. "Doing all right?" He spoke very loudly, and it was clear he was well on.

"Ay, I'm fine," said Shandon.

"Don't mind that chap that was in earlier. He doesn't mean any harm. Just a poor unfortunate sort of chap."

"Ay, it's no problem," said Shandon. The barman had the drinks ready—a gin and tonic and a white wine. The man handed over a fiver. "Would you like one yourself, Tom?"

"Thanks, I'll have a half-pint of lager," said Tom. He got the change and poured his own drink. "At the theatre again the night, Gordon?"

"That's right," said Gordon. He was poised, holding the drinks, about to walk back with them to the woman at the table. "Noel Coward, I think. Or was it Terence Rattigan? I can never remember. Mary would know."

"It was *Private Lives*," the woman in the blue dress called. Her voice was also loud and rich. "He knows perfectly well."

"Good was it?" asked the barman.

"Marvellous," she said.

"It was rubbish," said Gordon. He carried the drinks over and slid in beside her. They said nothing to each other, but started in on the drinks.

"Did you say you wanted something?" the barman asked Shandon.

"Eh, no, I'm just off." But he nursed the last of his beer for another few minutes. He'd no idea people still got dressed up to go to the theatre. Well, nobody did, except these two.

When the barman was away putting chairs on tables, he walked out.

It was cold. The sky was clear but he couldn't see many stars because of the glow of the city. He crossed over the street and was about to head off when something made him stop. It was the realisation that he was going back. He had resolved nothing. He wished the bar was open till two, or three. He'd stay there all night if he could.

He pulled his coat around him and rested on a wall. It was too cold to be hanging around, but still he waited. After a while he saw the old couple coming out of the bar. They stood for a moment, he looking up at the sky, she adjusting her stole. Then they began to walk, unsteadily, arm in arm along the pavement.

Shandon didn't move until the storm-doors of the bar, as if unassisted by human hand, swung shut. He heard the sound of bolts being shot home. The barman would probably leave by a back entrance. He thought about the man Mathieson, who had left twenty minutes earlier. Mathieson could be waiting for him, somewhere out here. Mathieson could be waiting for Shandon and Shandon could be waiting for Tom, the barman. It was an interesting scenario, all of them waiting in the shadows. But what would he be waiting for Tom for? Only after he had thought about it for a while, how it might have come about, only then did he push himself away from the wall and start to move. He had a fair walk ahead of him.

Facing It

Then one day he looked down between his legs and he knew it could no longer be avoided. He looked down and saw white and then the bowl filled red and dark and nothing solid in it at all and he knew something was very wrong. Just for a moment as he sat there in privacy his throat constricted and he thought he was going to cry. But he held that back at least. Everything else had failed him. He went through another quarter-roll of paper but he knew no amount of paper could staunch the flow now, the lemon-scented air-freshener had failed him and the open window, beyond these the attempt to keep an upright posture, the firm handshake and cutting out the whisky, even in the last few weeks a kind of muttered, embarrassed praying—more a plea really against the pain—everything had failed him, he knew it was all coming apart in there, it was breaking up into pieces and flowing out of him. He would have to go to the doctor but he would go without telling *her*. He could hear her busying herself in the kitchen as if she knew what was happening, but she didn't. He didn't want her to worry or be upset but when it came to the bit that was what would happen.

And the doctor would say, he could hear him saying, yes, it's very bad, I'm afraid it's very bad indeed, so maybe he wouldn't go there after all, maybe if he just gave himself a final wipe and flushed away all that stuff that was himself, flushed it twice and got himself on his feet and composed, deep breaths in the mirror, he could just call to her, not have to go into the kitchen at all, just call saying, I'm off out for a paper, and once outside turn left towards the park and then with the back held as straight as possible keep going, keep walking, walking, walking, through the park, through the city, through the suburbs, out towards the hills, as far as he could go until he dropped.

The End Is Nigh

Each day the limping man extends his sermon. It's like a word game where each player repeats a list, adding a new item at the end. "I went to the end of the world and I saw an Avalanche." "I went to the end of the world and I saw an Avalanche and a Ball of fire." "I went to the end of the world and I saw an Avalanche, a Ball of fire and a City in ruins." Only he is playing this game on his own. He limps past me or I stagger past him and each time he has another vision. It's as the poet said:

> "He was not a prophet crying in the wilderness,
>   but the wilderness cried in him."

This is what I think when I see him tramping the streets around the station.

"In these days a man went forth from the frontier, bearing his poor mouth and his tall staff, and his body like a broken reed, to fulfil a promise to himself, to make a journey he had always meant to make.

"He was not a prophet or an emissary; nor was he a spy. He had no flag to plant, nor claim to stake. He was a witness. His was not a voice crying in the wilderness, but the wilderness cried in him.

"He went to listen and to hear; to wander out among the past; to see what he could find."

He limps and he slavers, his jaw is unshaven and his trousers are tied with string. He has a wound upon his face that does not heal. Sometimes he carries a can of lager as if it were a collecting-tin. But it never rattles.

"Some thought him drunk, or that he was deranged. Others loathed his calm, his sense of purpose, the way he did not glance across his shoulder. Brats in broken shoes pursued him, mocking his tilt and twisting their faces in contempt of his stupidity. Soldiers spat upon his head and cursed his wish to go where they would never go, not for glory, not for wages, not for honour, not for freedom. Mothers, parodying vice, bared and thrust their thighs to him, and shrieked, and laughed and wept, and tore their hair, then turned away in rank despair to bargain with the soldiers. Their children hunkered in the stour, selecting missiles.

"All this convinced him only of his sanity; the crusts of concrete hurled at his back assured him that he faced the right direction. He hirpled on, into the north, alone."

He catches my eye as he passes, or I catch his. Whichever it is, he brings a start of fear and guilt to my senses. He is drunk or mad or both. I have a few coins in my pocket. He never asks for them, but he knows they are there. When our eyes meet I thrust my hand in deep, feeling for them with a sense of urgency.

"For it was terror that he left behind him, there in the fort without a wall. He could smell it, thick as the brown pollution sweating in the air—the concentrated fear of folk deserted by their own civilisation. Out beyond them, where they scarcely dared to look, were nameless things, unspeakable barbarities, and against their gathering these people were defenceless.

"Terror and ignorance, these were the twin pillars of their education. Successive governments assured them that the old wall to the south was to be resurrected, but they knew this to be a lie. They knew that each summer more and more of the stone was shipped away, ostensibly for restoration, never to return. Belief had long since crumbled, and yet they sat and faked bravado, scraped a living in outposts such as this, and dreamed of the retreat, of the order that would shunt them south behind the limit of their hope. Dream and dread together. If they could only put their faith in the north, for the north was deep in their faith. They spent their nights with videos and alcohol, each of the most violent kind.

"They were not Romans. They had no city to defend, no Capitol. Neither could they fall upon their swords."

The last factory is long closed. Middle-aged men have forgotten the meaning of work. Young men have never known it. The women slave at everything. They are resilient.

Sometimes I think he is drunk beyond repair. Sometimes he seems the soberest man on earth. I feel for the coins in my pocket when I pass him on my way to the counting-house. I feel for them on my way to the station, going home.

"The last factory was long closed. Far away into the half-light the last black drop of oil had been wrung from the gowly grey sea. The roads that ran from west to east and back again were bitten with frost and dense with weeds. Between the weathering and the terrorists they were beyond repair. Once sterile, these black ribbons were now the home of creatures which had learnt new ways: foxes and wild dogs and carrion-crows. Elsewhere the rivers were sewers and the lochs were stanks.

"From the once-proud towers that had promised hope, now bruised and grey and crumbling, the savage moor stretched forth, desolate, cold, half moss-hags and half concrete and cable. Where people had once escaped to pray, now wild men roamed.

"Beyond lay the great strangled forests, the mutant jungles of Lochaber, the howling rainwoods of Moidart, the night-worlds of tall evergreens thick with the screams of banshees and baboons. In Badenoch the wolves and wildcats were no more, but strange, shaggy lions were rumoured.

"All these things were uncertain, but he had kept them and pondered them in his heart. None who had gone to the north had ever returned."

The counting-house is where I spend my day. I would not call it a job—a dangerous word which can be taken from you in a moment. I would call it a safe place to be. As safe as there is anyway. Each afternoon when I leave I rush gratefully to the nearest bar and drink as much as I can before the last train home. This is what I have come to.

"Also it was said of these days that they were the end of days, that history, age, antiquity, time itself, were riding up the wheel, reclaiming the future, rolling the continents up like carpets and through toothless, slavered gums sucking all the world, even this poor wretched land, into a vortex of oblivion. But he did not believe it. He did not believe in turning back."

The limping man shouts at me. He bars my path, his stance halfway between a stoop and a crouch. Either he is about to fold to the pavement or to pounce. "These are the days!" he shouts, showering me with grey and brown spittle. "These are the days that are the end of days! The end of time! Time—sucking on itself!"

I am walking along a rough path through a wood. The sun throws shafts of light clashing down upon the hard earth through the branches of the trees. A man stands in my path. He carries a long sword and his chest swells beneath a great breastplate of burnished steel. He says, "This is my fortress and you shall not pass."

I say to him, "Where is your fortress?" and the man's arm extends over the ground as if he were sowing seed, and rises to the trees and falls again.

"Here," he says. "Here I built it and here I stand."

"I see nothing," I say.

"Look," says the warrior, and he reaches with his free hand to the nearest tree and touches the air beside it. Then for a brief moment I do indeed see the stonework among the leaves, and that the warrior stands beneath an arch that is not the branches meeting overhead but a kind of portal made of stone. And I reach out with the tip of my staff and touch the portal, and it collapses all around him. And the warrior falls upon the ground and weeps, a terrible, wretched sound. And I pass through the ruins of his folly, and hirple on, into the north, alone.

The Mountain

For more than half a year David lived in a dream. Days drifted into days, weeks filled to months, and then two seasons had slipped by and spring was there. High on the mountain great crescents of snow still hung on the rims of the corries, or shrank from the sun in shaded patches, but down at the house there were daffodils and primroses, and everywhere the crying of lambs. He began to shake himself of the greyness and the damp.

He had been so lethargic. Constructiveness had seemed beyond him. He did the bits of work that were necessary; cashed the benefit cheques and the occasional cheques from his mother at the store which was also the post office; gathered wood; made the peats and coals last. Often he didn't get up till the afternoon—to save on fuel was his excuse to himself. But really it was because dozing, waking, dozing again, was what he did best.

There were no beasts left—they'd all been sold after his grandfather died. But even before that it was only sheep, and Willie MacRae, a neighbouring crofter, had tended them on the old man's behalf. Old Willie ran his own sheep on the croft now—which was good; better, at any rate, than letting the land go. But for David it meant there was no reason for work, just the house to be looked after. And that didn't take much with only himself there.

Almost every week Janet came to see him. The bus took an hour from Ullapool and arrived at the road end at four in the afternoon, and there wasn't one back until the next day at eleven. So she would have to stay, and sometimes she'd stay for two nights. On the intervening day they mightn't go out at all, just sit by the fire and read, talk, doze. She'd have stayed longer if it hadn't been for her gran. Her mam worked in the school at Ullapool, cleaning, and two days was as long as her gran could last without someone going in to prepare another series of meals, tidy the house up and give her a bath. She was fine, the granny, she was a hundred per cent all there in the head, but she found it tough getting from room to room, let alone going out. Janet said it was like part-time work, only it wasn't recognised as such. She didn't grudge her gran though, and it was one thing less for her mam. In the absence of any paid work, it gave a semblance of structure to her week.

Structure was something completely lacking for David in this period. Even her visits didn't give him that, since there wasn't a phone and she'd just turn up. That was fine, he liked it that way. He knew she'd always be back. In the summer he'd come alive again. There'd be work in the hotel if he wanted it.

They were just friends. Folk wouldn't have believed it but it was true. They didn't sleep together; they shared each other's company. Folk weren't daft, they knew fine what they were up to. But they weren't up to anything. She liked the feeling she got when she visited, being there with him. It was like hibernation.

Still, in spite of the lethargy, it wasn't true what was said about the place—what was said about places like it all over the Highlands—that time slowed down there. Time went by just as fast, you just didn't notice it so much. You lost track a wee bit but the pace didn't drop. What was different was the quietness. On cold, clear days when the wind fell, he'd walk by the sea and then it did seem as though you could measure time passing in the silence. In a town, with traffic and shouting voices and all the other background noise, time wouldn't be heard, although you'd always be seeing it, checking your watch, watching the clock. Here you could pick up the sound of it, still going by you at the same speed, and not see it at all.

He read a lot. Janet would bring books, and he had a few shelves of books of his own, most of which he read for a second or third time. The afternoons and the evenings were for reading. And he listened to the radio, tuning in to different stations, never knowing what he would find. He listened to the news, plays, documentaries, the shipping forecast. The voices came out of the air into the black box and out again to him. He could go for days at a stretch and not say a word.

The store was a mile away and only opened from ten till four when the tourists weren't around. The Englishman who owned it left his assistant Helen Mackay to run it for most of the winter. He wouldn't have bothered himself, but it was in the terms of the post office franchise, and the scattering of locals needed the shop for basics like milk and bread. The odd one like David who had no car needed it for everything. The choice was sparse, although Helen would get things in specially if you ordered them. He ate cauliflower and cheese sauce a lot; and tatties; and big soups that sat on the stove for days, thickening and crusting with every heat.

"Ay, David, and how's all with you?"

"Fine, Helen. Yourself?"

"Oh, the usual. We were down at the hotel last night, Angus and me, just for a drink. We were looking for you but we never saw you."

"No, I've not been out much—can't afford the prices, you know."

"Well, we would always stand you a drink."

"That's good of you but I like to pay my way."

"Och, well, no doubt we'll catch you some time."

Everybody knew who he was, but nobody knew him except Janet, and she was from Ullapool. And they thought they knew about her too, getting off the bus and walking up the road to the croft every week, staying over, but they didn't. They had David marked down for a townie come to find his roots, and Janet for his girlfriend. He'd be off with the first bad snow, as soon as the road was cleared, that's what they said. But he wasn't. They didn't know a thing.

Helen was the exception, she stuck up for him, she'd taken a liking to him and felt he was different. Not that he was a breath of fresh air exactly, he was too faded and tired-looking to be that. Maybe it was that tiredness, when he was young enough to be her son, that made her feel—not sorry for him, but interested in him. She gave him a good word whenever she could.

So then they changed their tune, the rest of them, they said it must be his grandfather's blood in him that kept him there. His father didn't have the blood, but maybe the boy did. The boy— he was twenty-six! Not that he'd get much done, they said—the croft was in a state, hadn't been worked properly for years because the old man hadn't been able, and anyway what did the boy know about crofting? No, it was all going back to nature in spite of the sheep, like most of the other places in the township as the people aged, back to nature or to the English, and if he went away and the iron on the roof wasn't sorted that would be the end of it. If the lassie stopped coming on the bus he'd go and that would be it. The family would be daft not to sell to incomers, there'd be plenty who'd take it for a summer home, and pay a good price too. Then there'd be one less roof to go over the heads of the young who might have stayed. But would they have stayed anyway? Not likely, the young ones!

Early on, before he settled, David used to take the bus to Ullapool himself once a week. Doing the trip that way round, you could go in the morning, spend two or three hours there and come back in the afternoon. He'd fool himself into thinking he was going to look for boots, or a jumper, when in fact he was going because he wanted to see some different faces. It was a busy place, with the ferries to Lewis and the factory ships, but the town itself seemed to be dominated by incomers, the shops and cafes and B&Bs owned and run by them. It was funny how he didn't consider himself an incomer. He didn't think he stood out, or that he was easily spotted. But he was.

"Hello, David."

"Janet! What are you doing here?"

"I stay here, remember?"

"Oh, ay, with your mam."

"What about yourself?"

He told her about the croft, his granda dying, how his father didn't know what to do with it. His father who had left when he was seventeen, gone to university and trained to be a doctor, and who was never coming back. David wasn't working, his parents were driving him daft trying to get him to join the bank or the police or the civil service or any other organisation they thought respectable, so he told them he'd come up and look after the place for the winter. Janet and he had met the previous year, working in a bar in Edinburgh. Neither of them could afford the Edinburgh rents on the pay they got, and the hours and conditions were lousy. They'd both gone back home.

She was getting her gran's messages. They went for a drink that became two, then four. There'd been nothing between them in Edinburgh but here it was different. They weren't working together. They had made each other laugh and they still did. When he went for the bus they kissed and she said she'd come and see him. He warned her, he said, "You'll not get back the same day." "Is that a threat or a promise?" she said.

That was the level they were at. The possibility was always there but all winter it stayed just a possibility. Maybe they just liked fooling everybody else. Anything more would be a threat or a promise and they weren't in the mood for either.

Raymond Carver wrote about a kind of writing that described only a desert landscape—"a few dunes and lizards here and there, but no people; a place uninhabited by anything recognizably human. . . ." Such writing wasn't acceptable, Carver said, it alienated the reader. Any story had to have human interest. But was it even possible to write a story without human interest?

David discounted stories about animals living in societies—where they made decisions and had emotions like humans, twitching their noses to indicate displeasure, that kind of thing. Cuddly, simple, earnest rubbish. These stories weren't about animals at all. Then there was science fiction written entirely about robots or Martians, but this ran into the same difficulty—the robots had been built and programmed by humans, and the Martians were simply humans in another guise. All extra-terrestrials were depicted by an implicit contrasting of their characteristics with human characteristics. This was understandable. What other points of reference could there be?

The desert landscape David had in mind was up on the

mountain. But if he were to write about that he would simply be describing, not narrating a story. There would be no progression, or only of a particular kind. Desolation. Bitter cold. Snow falls. It freezes. More snow. Wind blows. The snow is shaped. Daylight barely illuminates the place. Night. Fierce wind, sleet, snow, ice. Insects trapped in crystals. Snow buntings search and feed. Eagle climbs the sky. Hare goes from brown to white, to brown. Eagle banks, sweeps, dives. Dotterels arrive in spring. Snow melts.

Then the climbers. The summer visitors. But they were there, the experienced ones, in the winter too. And even if you thought about the mountain without climbers on it, it still wasn't a dehumanised landscape. Even if you ignored the track, the cairns, the trig point. The desolation, after all, was in contrast to the cultivation below. The description was human. If it was true to say that what happened to him was irrelevant to the mountain but that what happened to the mountain was not irrelevant to him, nevertheless it was the saying of it that gave it its truth. The mountain revealed nothing but what humans took from it.

He'd climbed it in October, before the winter-long snow fell on it. He was not experienced and he went alone—this was before Janet started to visit. He didn't take risks, he went by the route that was dull but safe. But he knew, as he began to wake in the spring, that he was going to have to do it again, and go by the ridge, the hard way. He'd wait for a good day, and then he'd go.

He'd climbed the mountain once, though. Why should he do it again, that way or any way?

Why?

Because it would be more spectacular, more challenging, more strenuous, hence more rewarding?

These were all reasons. But why climb it at all?

Because if he didn't he wouldn't even think to ask the question. He wouldn't lift his eyes above the level of existence he was at. He'd spent the winter thinking about how he'd come to be there, at the foot of the mountain, now he was raising his aspirations.

There was a story he'd heard. He wasn't sure but thought it was
Chinese. Call it Chinese. He told it to Janet.

In the heart of China lived a young man called Yan who
wanted to see the sea. His home was a thousand miles inland,
but his greatest wish in life was to see the sea. He went to the
official in charge of travel permits.

"I want to see the sea," said Yan.

"Why do you want to do that?"

"It's just something I have to do. Here I am living in the
middle of this land, and there's a place as full of water as this
place is empty of it—fuller. This is amazing to me. I want to see
it."

"It is not necessary for you to see the sea," said the official.

"I know," said Yan, "but I just want to see it."

"I want? This is loose talk, Yan. Your desire is extravagant.
The sea will be there whether you see it or not."

"Yes, yes, but if I don't go I won't see it with my own eyes.
This is what is important."

"It seems important to you. But it is not important to the sea,
the land, or any other person. Do you doubt the existence of the
sea? Is the word of others, of your teachers, not enough?"

"It's not that I don't believe. My knowledge of the sea comes
from them. It is something remote, and yet they have made it a
part of my life. All I want to do is confirm it for myself."

The official saw that Yan was very determined. He explained
to him how inconvenient his desire was: how much it would cost
in terms of his lost labour, and the labour of others on the
railway, in towns along the journey, at the coast itself, for Yan
to see the sea. He tried to persuade Yan that his desire was
unpatriotic.

Yan said that this was not so. If he could see the sea once in
his life, he would see China in reality as he could only imagine
it now. This would make him understand and love his country
more.

But the official knew that once Yan understood one thing, he would want to understand another. There was a subjective way of looking at this, which was Yan's way, and an objective way, which was the official's. There was reason and there was feeling. Yan was thinking with feeling.

The official told Yan this and was about to refuse him permission to travel when Yan interrupted him:

"The philosopher Hume, however, says that reason is, and ought always to be, the slave of feelings, or, as he calls them, the passions. He says it is impossible for the passions to be opposed by, or contradictory to, truth and reason."

The official was surprised that Yan knew anything about Hume. He said:

"In the first place, Hume also points out that society functions only through the regulation of the passions by reason. In the second place, Hume is a Westerner, originating in a tiny, wet country which is plunged in darkness for half the year. . . ."

"Hold on," said Janet, "this isn't a Chinese story at all."

"You're right," said David. "I lied. I thought the name Yan gave it away. Could that be a Chinese name?"

"Can you not give us the Scottish version then?"

"No. But I can give you the Chinese version of another Scottish story."

This happened long ago in China, long before the Communists. There was this village that had once been ruled by a powerful family, but the family had married into an even more powerful family that ruled the neighbouring province. The big fortress above the village was empty eleven months of the year, and was only used when some of the family came on hunting trips, and to begin with the village was left pretty much to itself: the villagers looked after their own affairs, paid the taxes that were due, and almost forgot that the family still owned all of the land. But then one day word came that the annual tax on their houses was to be doubled. The village was to get nothing back in return, it was simply that their rulers needed more money to finance their extravagant life-style. The villagers went to the local sage, a very old man with a long straggly beard, and asked him what

84

they should do.

"What do you mean, what should you do?" he said.

"Well, this tax is completely unjust, and we'll have to starve to raise the money. Should we pay it, or should we rebel?"

"It is not for me to say if you should pay it," said the sage. "But certainly this is not the time to rebel."

So the villagers went away and with great hardship paid the new tax, unhappy and angry.

The next year word came that a third of all the village's cows were required by their rulers, and must be driven to the city. The villagers were outraged. They went back to the old man.

"Should we not refuse this decree and rise up?" they demanded.

"No," said the sage, "now is not the time to rise up."

The next year the rulers wanted every third sack of corn to be sent to the city. The villagers went again to the old man and told him about it.

"Surely we must arm ourselves and rise against these thieves," they said.

"No," he said, "now is not the time."

The next year the rulers wanted to tax the water from the river. Every gallon of water that was used would be taxed. The villagers were about to seek the old man's advice again, when one of the younger men said:

"Look, year after year we go to that old fellow and ask him what we should do. And year after year he tells us that we should do nothing. What's the point of asking him? I say we should march to the city, us and the people of all the other villages, and say we refuse to give any more to these parasites."

And that was what they did. They took what weapons they had, and joined with the other oppressed people of the country-side, and marched on the city. And not only did the ruling family give in to their demands, but the people of the city also rose up, and the family was overthrown, and all the injustices corrected.

So then the villagers returned to the village, and they went to the old man and berated him. "You old fool," they said, "you always told us not to rise up, so we took your advice, and it did us no good at all. So this time we acted for ourselves and ignored you, and now look—we have been victorious and won back our freedom. How do you account for your stupidity?"

"Oh," said the old man, "the stupidity was not mine, but yours. Every time you came seeking my advice or approval to rebel, you proved that you were not ready to do so. The time that you did not come to me, that was the time to rise up. But of course you didn't need me to tell you that."

"That," said David, "is the parable of the not yet sufficiently oppressed."

"What are you saying?" said Janet. "Not that old folk are full of crap and shouldn't be listened to, you're not saying that?"

"No. I'm saying people must empower themselves, nobody else will do it for them. Leaders won't fight the battles. They'll only lead if they're pushed to the front."

But there was another problem. Were the Scots being oppressed? Were they *really* being oppressed? Surely they were with the oppressors. How could they pretend otherwise, that they hadn't been the colonists, the empire-builders, and that now they didn't exploit the people of other countries with their comparative wealth, keep them in poverty and debt, guzzle up the world's resources? How could it be denied?

It couldn't be. There was no excuse. It had to be acknowledged.

Then what *was* the excuse? For all the crap? Scotland was like some hopelessly inadequate liberal in therapy, full of self-pity while all around the landscape was in flames. If it was oppressed why didn't it do something about it?

"Why do we think we're so special? So put upon? So great? So wee? So brilliant? So awful? Why do we feel the need to boast about dozens of great inventors on tea-towels, for God's sake? On tea-towels!"

"But you know fine well there are different levels and different methods of oppression," said Janet. "And that sometimes people conspire in their own degradation."

It was true, and when he saw the truth of what she said he wanted to include himself—and her—among the victims, but as

86

soon as he tried the same voice spoke up again. Guilt. What right have I to complain about my life? About the political condition I'm in? My life is a fairy-tale compared to the horror stories some people live. All over the world the horror was going on. He was living at the end of the twentieth century in utter luxury compared to every previous age. Not only did he live in a country free from war, pestilence, famine and natural disaster, within that country he enjoyed the privileges of being white, male, able-bodied and educated. If he wasn't employed he at least had a choice of roofs over his head, including this one where he could be completely on his own if he wanted to. That was being in control of his life in a way most people could hardly even imagine. And even if the worst befell him, or one like him, even if, say, he was kidnapped and kept in chains and darkness in the cellars of West Beirut for six years, there would still be this to return to and that experience to measure against it, even to exploit. But for others there was no escape, no end. Elsewhere there were permanent, constant horrors going on that he could not begin to comprehend. There were men and women in South America who were beaten senseless in the corridors of football stadia turned into slaughterhouses, tortured with water and electricity and fire, then put against a blood-stained wall and shot. There were whole families wiped out in a tidal wave of mud in Bangladesh, their bodies washed up bloated and broken like parcels of meat to decay in the sun, to become nothing more than a stinking danger to the lives of others. There were whole regions of Africa where to be alive meant simply that you were almost certain to die of malnutrition. There were people being tortured and starved and persecuted and dying of AIDS and cancer and violence and little children wasting away with dysentery and typhoid every second of every day. What conceivable right had he to be discontented, to think that life was unfair?

And even here, in this country, he was at or near the pinnacle of good fortune. Every day on the streets of Edinburgh he had seen the rest: the thirty-five-year-old man with the seventy-year-old face who haunted the bus station—returned to the so-called

87

community because asylum had become a dirty word—bloody and bowed, permanently clutching a can of Special Brew, articulating in a long low continuous moan the misery of his existence; the scuffed, drip-nosed shuffle of thieves hooked on glue or heroin scouring the shops for whatever easily lifted goods would pay for the next hit, who would be dead by Christmas because if the habit didn't kill them the cold would; the women left to deal with the wreckage not just of their own damp, torn, wretched lives but those of their redundant husbands, their unemployable sons and pregnant daughters and all their poor wee shit-scared pee-the-bed bastard bairns. That was what he saw from his place near the top of the hill and because he knew it was a snapshot, capturing all the stereotyped grime of the people at the bottom and none of their graces, he felt guilty. He was being bought off, he was being acquiescent. None of it was his fault but it made him feel guilty and feeling guilty was supposed to make you feel grateful for what you had but deep down he knew it shouldn't be like that for anyone and that thinking like this wasn't going to make any of it any better.

Worse. A man terrorised and beat his Filipino wife for years, then murdered her, chopped her up and cooked her because this was cheaper than the divorce she finally told him she was going to get. A man paid another man to throw sulphuric acid at his estranged wife, blinding her and destroying her face. A man in social work raped the children given into his care. How can I, he thought, feel mistreated or hurt?

A man held hostage in Iraq before the war against Saddam Hussein came home changed forever, fearful and depressed. Six months later he took his 12-bore shotgun into the garage and shot himself. His wife found him. In his pocket was a note: "I cannot muck up your life for another day. . . . May God forgive me." God forgive *him*! The tragedy and pain could not be contained by such words, such small, few words. My life, *my* life is a beautiful gift alongside this.

This was why he was here. He had come to understand, over the winter, that this was why he had ended up on the croft. He'd had a kind of breakdown, not a nervous one but a social one.

He'd had to come here to work himself through it.

"Do you mind Sanni?" he asked Janet.

"Of course," she said.

"Mind how he got stabbed?"

"How could I not? Just walking home one night after we'd shut the pub, just going home. He could have been killed."

"Ay, and we all used to walk home late at night from that place. But Sanni was the one because he was black."

"It makes you want to throw up," she said. "Hearing that the next day made me feel like I'd done it."

Once David was walking with Sanni, before the stabbing, and not late at night in the city either. They'd gone to Sutherland and crossed from the Tongue road over the hills to the east coast. It was a two-day walk, and they carried rucksacks, with sleeping-bags and a tent. The first day it rained all morning, then brightened up as they rounded a long loch probably teeming with fish. A couple of boats were tied up at a wooden jetty, near the end of a rough track. There would be parties of sportsmen here at times, paying top rates for the privilege.

They saw nobody that day. They camped a mile or two beyond the loch, cooked a meal, and were up about six the next morning, walking hard to get away from clouds of midges. About eleven, they passed a lodge and got onto a wider track. They could see a vehicle coming towards them, a Japanese four-wheel drive lurching around on the rough surface. It stopped in front of them and as they tried to pass on the driver's side the door swung open, blocking the gap between motor and ditch. A huge figure in green heaved out and closed the door. There was another, slighter figure in the passenger seat.

"Where are you two going then?" The keeper's accent was local.

David pointed facetiously down the track. "Eh, we're going that way."

"I can see that. What are you doing?"

"Just walking."

"Disturbing the deer no doubt, and the grouse."

"We saw some deer this morning. About a mile away. Can you disturb them at that kind of distance?"

"You're very smart, aren't you?" The passenger had by this time slid out on his side. His eyes were fixed on Sanni.

"Did you ask permission to walk through here?" he said. His voice was thinner and drier than the keeper's, and, if not English, near enough as made no difference.

"Ay," said Sanni. David looked at him sharply, it was the first he'd heard of it. "And we got it tae," said Sanni.

Both the keeper and the gentry stared coldly at Sanni. It was bad enough finding a black man on your land, but one that spoke like a keelie was too much.

"Did you?" said the gentry disbelievingly.

"Ay," said Sanni. "I got it fae him, and he got it fae me."

"The grouse season's about to start, and the culling's already begun, did you consider that?"

"Look," said David. "We're on the path. We're not doing any damage, we're just walking through. So get out the bloody road."

"This is my road," said the gentry. "My road and my land."

"Bollocks," said Sanni.

Afterwards, David realised that, short of resorting to violence or racial abuse, there wasn't much answer to that. The keeper might be up for it, but not his boss. But at the time he found himself torn between fear and an intense desire to laugh. If Sanni had started to protest in Gaelic the situation couldn't have been more bizarre. As if in a dream, David followed on behind as Sanni pushed past.

"Don't think about stopping to put your tent up!" the keeper shouted.

"Naw, we did that yesterday," said Sanni. "Set fire tae the heather tae! Wi a fiery cross, ken!" But it was lost on them.

"Weird, in't it?" said Sanni. "I'm black and scotticised— born and brought up here. That guy's white and anglicised. And I'm the intruder."

Three months later he was stuck with a knife in Leith Walk.

David chapped at Willie MacRae's door. Willie's sheep were on his granda's croft. Whenever he went by in his tractor he raised his hand and David waved back, but communication hadn't got beyond that. Helen Mackay said there had been a time when David's granda and Willie had been good friends, but the old man had got very religious in his last years and there had been arguments about Willie working on a Sunday. "The trouble was, your grandad was dependent on Willie at the end. It would hurt your pride, that. He was old but Willie's not that young himself. Ay, he was a proud man, your grandad."

It was Mrs MacRae that came to the door. "Come in, come in." He was sat down and had to wait patiently while the weather was talked through before he could explain what he'd come for.

"There's a sheep lying on its back down by the shore. I tried to right it but it just fell over again."

"Och, well, you'll need to show himself where it is. I doubt it'll just be needing a jag to put it on its feet."

They had a cup of tea till Willie came in. "Don't take your boots off," his wife called when she heard him at the back of the house. "There's a sheep sick that David here's been telling us about."

He rode back on the tractor, standing behind the seat, looking down at the leathery white-haired neck of Willie below his bunnet. "And how are you keeping?" yelled Willie above the tractor's roar.

The sheep was still there. David stood back while the old man had a look at her. "Can we get her up out of this hole a wee bittie?" Willie said. David held the beast between his knees while it struggled feebly, and Willie injected it.

"Now we'll see her," he said. They watched for a few minutes. Quite suddenly the sheep stood up, shook itself and wandered off.

"The staggers," said Willie. "She was lacking magnesium in the grass. That's what I gave her. Thank you for that," he added.

"No problem," said David. The phrase had Willie looking puzzled. "You know," David went on, "if there was ever any work I could do, to help you like, I'd be happy to."

The hint of a smile flickered over Willie's lips. "Och, well," was all he said. It was as if David had been too presumptuous in asking.

But again, over the noise of the tractor, when he dropped David back at the house, the shy smile played on his face. "I have a dram sometimes in the evening if you were ever passing."

"This is all very well," said Janet, "but what are *we* going to do?"

"I don't know," said David. "I don't know at all, if you're talking about *us*."

So it was coming to this at last: how much longer could they go on without the promise or the threat? What was to be the level of their being together? Ah, the old folks were right all along. It always was going to come to this.

"Well, what are *you* going to do? Here, with the croft? *Find* yourself? And then go back to Edinburgh, Glasgow ... London ... America? Are you going to let your dad sell the place?"

"Well, what are the possibilities of staying here? What can I do? Be a crofter? Be a writer? These are romantic but not likely options. I could probably work behind the bar at the hotel in the summer, I've got the experience. We both have, come to think of it. It'd be doing someone else out of a job, but it might be a start. No, no it wouldn't. But I can't imagine what other kind of life I could live here. Myself, I mean, realistically. Some huge leap of imagination is required which I cannot make. I could be a crofter if Angus would teach me, or Willie MacRae. I could go and ask him and he'd say, what would you want to do that for? He'd tell me there's not enough on the croft to make a decent living and he only does it because he's too old to stop. Or maybe I could be a fish-farmer or a drystane-dyker or something, one of these couthy, folksy jobs. Or better, I could do something unexpected, new, entirely viable but still in keeping with where I am. I could create a change in living against the landscape without affecting the landscape. I don't know what that would be but I could do it. Look at me, Janet, I'm clutching at straws.

I don't want to waste my life. The old folks think we're afraid to get our hands dirty, the likes of you and me, they think we're afraid of hard work, but we're not. We want to get stuck into something that means something. We want to work but we don't want to be wage-slaves. But we need someone to show us how, that's what we need."

"Nobody's going to show us. Nobody'll organise that for us. We'll have to do it for ourselves."

"That's one of the things the government has achieved in the last fifteen years. They've broken down any sense of continuity in work. Young people don't have a proper working relationship with old people. All kinds of traditions have gone with that. Not just skills, but traditions of mutual respect, mutual strength, mutual self-defence. There's no continuity of the idea of resistance any more."

"I don't think that's true," said Janet. "But if it is, it's just another thing we're going to have to relearn. You've got all the ideas, David, you're just lacking the moment to act."

"What about you?" he asked.

"Well, I've got my gran, and my mam. That's something. But it's not enough. It doesn't satisfy. My expectations have been raised. There are so many possibilities. Nothing anyone can do will alter that."

They watched the sun sink into a flat calm sea. The sky glowed red, a good sign. Later, across the red glow of the fire, she handed him a sheet of paper and a pen. "Write down as many reasons as you can think of why you want to climb this mountain again. The hard way, by the ridge."

He had an image of them scrambling up that black spine together, tiny against the skyline, edging their way towards the summit, and on either side of them the snow and rock dropping away for hundreds of feet. Just before he started writing she added, "And 'because it's there' doesn't count."

After a minute he had this:

1. To prove to myself I can do it.
2. To say I've done it.

93

3. For the view.
4. To have a day to remember.
5. To stay fit.
6.

"What's at 6?" she asked.

"Don't know. It's something else."

The day before, in the store, he'd mentioned to Helen that he'd be going up the mountain the first clear day there was. "What are you wanting to go up there for?" she'd said, only half-joking. "There's plenty of low-lying ground for you."

"What's at 6?" Janet repeated.

He had to think about it. It wasn't easy to know what should be there.

"It's something that happens at the tops of mountains. Nowhere else. There's nowhere further you can go, without taking flight."

She said, "You always think you'll remember what it's like up there, but you never do. You always have to go back."

After a while she said:

"And there's another thing. This country, it always seems so huge from the tops of mountains, and yet from the tops of mountains you can see how small it really is."

And much later, lying in front of the fire, she murmured:

"Tell me another story."

"Now?"

"Now."

"No, later."

"Now no later," she said, half-asleep.

"Tomorrow," he said. "Tomorrow we climb the mountain."

What Love Is

Something in the light changes, and Dan, who is not long home from his work, realises it has started to snow. He goes from the kitchen to the front room of the flat and stands at the bay window, looking down on the traffic and the orange glow of the streetlights. A small thrill shivers through him as he watches the first flakes pass by. It's like being a child again. A gust of wind blows the snow upwards, and the falling flakes mix with the rising. Dan looks into the cloud-laden sky over the grey city. He sees it as a great sagging mattress stuffed with tiny feathers. The mattress has burst and there are feathers everywhere. He looks at his watch. It's half-past five. He thinks about Joan coming back on the bus through the snow, but she won't leave her work until after seven. He has a couple of hours.

Amazing what you can see through windows. Once, through this very one, he saw a woman fly. She lived on the other side of the street, on the other side of the constant stream of cars and taxis and buses, in a fourth-floor flat. She cleaned her windows by climbing out on the ledge and holding on to the frame while she wiped and polished. Forty feet above the traffic she stood on a ledge six inches wide, and Dan could hardly bear to look at her. He closed his eyes because she frightened him, balancing there, and he saw the arc of her body falling backwards and being held like a sheet of paper in the air and then suddenly her gift of flight—this being the only way to save her—and when he opened his eyes again the window was closed and the woman gone.

Another time, he was washing his breakfast things in the kitchen sink before leaving for work, and across the back-greens he saw a young woman doing the same, directly opposite but one floor down. As his hands moved in the bowl of soapy water he saw her stop and lower her head. She was wearing a white blouse and he saw her fingers, which must, like his, have been wet, go to touch the front of it. Then she reached for a towel, wiped her hands, and swiftly unbuttoning the blouse she slipped it off. She must have spilt something on it, coffee or marmalade or something. She held a corner of the towel under the tap for a moment, and he watched her dab at the blouse with it. He imagined the tops of her breasts curving out of her bra—it was too far for him to really see this—her hair falling forward, her breasts rising and falling as she worked at the stain—even through two lots of glass she seemed very alive to him. After a minute she held the blouse up to the light, then draped it over one arm and left the room. Tears sprang into Dan's eyes. He was leaning hard up against the sink unit. He took his wet hand away from himself. Sex. That was what he wanted. He couldn't, though. He couldn't go back to bed. He couldn't wake Joan because she was on the late shift and would want another hour's sleep. He felt guilty because in any case he didn't want to have sex with Joan, he wanted it with a woman across the way, in another room in another flat in another life.

Dan isn't frightened of other lives. He imagines them all the time. The only life he is frightened of is his own.

Every morning, whether she is on the early shift or the late one, Joan takes a bus to her work. She works from eight till five or ten till seven, and she does a morning every third Saturday as well. She would drive to work if they owned a car, but they can't afford one. She learned to drive when she was eighteen, in her father's car, and she passed her test first time. She needs this skill for her job. She works on the reservations desk of a car-hire firm. Self-drive, to use the jargon. She has to be able to drive the cars from one area of the forecourt to another, and park them in confined spaces. The self-drive desk is only one part of the place, which is a big Ford dealer's. There is a showroom for new models and a parking-lot full of secondhand ones, and there is the self-drive desk. Joan has been there for fifteen years.

Other lives disturb Joan. The bus is full of them, different ones at different times of the day, and when she finds herself thinking about them she does her best to block them out. She doesn't want them to encroach. Her life may not be perfect but it is hers and she has it worked out, the routine of it. The routine is what keeps her going; she will not allow it to oppress her.

"How was your day?" Dan asks her. He is cutting up vegetables for tea. He cooks the tea on the days when she is on the late shift.

"Just the usual," she says. Once—only once—Dan went to see her at her work. It was a summer afternoon and he decided to walk at least part of the way home. It wasn't much of a detour to go by the Ford dealer's place. Afterwards he wished he hadn't. There were three women on the self-drive desk, Joan and two others. They were dealing with five customers and all the phones were ringing. The women were making bookings, taking money or credit cards, inspecting driving-licences, explaining the insurance, checking that returned cars had full tanks, taking customers to their cars and demonstrating the controls to them. Whenever they got out from behind the desk they seemed to be about to break into a run. Their manner was polite, efficient and subservient. All of the customers were men. Dan stood just inside the door watching this scene for a few minutes, without Joan seeing him. Thirty feet away, a couple of sharp-suited salesmen were standing about in the showroom. They were doing nothing, and seemed oblivious to the frantic activity of the women. Occasionally one of them would run his finger along the roof or bonnet of one of the new cars, as if to demonstrate his expertise, his familiarity with the merchandise. They paid Dan no attention because he did not look like someone with the money to buy a car. This was true. Several of the models on display cost more than his entire year's salary. He quietly left before Joan saw him. He never mentioned to her that he had been there.

"Just the usual," she says, and Dan is horrified and ashamed that his wife has done that job for fifteen years. He chops the carrots with a vengeance.

Yvonne at his work keeps lecturing him, in a friendly, good-intentioned way. "You're too willing," she tells him. "You're too conscientious. Nobody should have to put up with the amount of work they give you."

Yvonne herself is no slacker. She's the receptionist. Apart from not having to deal with the cars, her job is as frantic as Joan's. She fields the phone-calls and the visitors and does some typing and she even finds time to give Dan advice. She is twenty-two—half his age—but she doesn't see any irony in giving advice to a man old enough to be her father. Dan's official job-title is Requisitions Manager. The firm—a small but industrious firm of architects—gave him this name and a ten per cent rise after he'd been with them for five years and Storeman had become too much of an under-statement to be ignored. As well as running the stores, Dan is in charge of repairs, equipment, the post-room, and health and safety. He is responsible for the maintenance and cleaning contracts and the stationery purchases, and often he acts as a courier, delivering documents to other locations in the city. When he has a spare half-hour he'll sometimes work the switchboard to let Yvonne get on with something else. He is indispensable to the firm, and this gives him enough satisfaction to offset the nagging feeling that he is underpaid and overworked. Yvonne, who is not long out of college and is afraid of no one, fuels his suspicions. "They take advantage of your good nature," she says. "They exploit you, you know they do. You shouldn't let them."

Dan at home. He has a big record collection. He loves the sound of a woman singing, and it doesn't much matter to him if it's Jessye Norman or Mary Black or Nina Simone. There's something about any woman's voice which is worth listening to. That's what he thinks. But most of all he listens to Billie Holiday. He could listen to her sing for hours and think only minutes had gone by. He has about twenty different albums of Billie Holiday, many of them with different recordings of the same song, little variations that he has become totally familiar with—so that he can listen to a song and say, "Yes, with Ray Ellis and his orchestra, 1958 sessions." Joan likes Billie Holiday too, but she gets irritated by this perfectionism. "Sometimes I think you don't listen to the songs themselves any more. You listen for the bits that are missing." Dan gives her his smile, the one that says, yes, you're right, but you don't know anything. "You don't know," Billie sings, "what love is, until you've learned the meaning of the blues." What a life, thinks Dan, alone in the front room at two in the morning, what a life she had to have, to sing like that.

Joan sits on the bus and different lives come at her, veering away at the last moment. She tries to be untouched by them, but it's hard. One morning there are three Asian girls going into town. Their hair is thick and black—she can imagine how heavy it must feel just by looking at it—but their loose black silk trousers look lightweight. Although young they seem very dignified, aloof even. She is not a racist, but she is sure of one thing: their lives and hers have nothing in common.

Another time, coming home in the evening, it's three white girls. They are loud but at the same time conspiratorial, trying to impress the bus with their grown-up talk, which is about the different stages of undress they have reached with their boy-friends. Joan, who could be their mother, is embarrassed and intrigued. She can't stop herself listening. Then a woman of her own age stands to get off the bus, and as she passes the girls her rage comes pouring out: "You're disgusting! Decent people having to listen to your filth! Dog-dirt! You're worse than dog-dirt!" "Piss off!" the girls chorus as she steps off the bus. Joan finds herself turning to watch the woman disappear on the crowded pavement.

One day there's an old drunk man giving the world view to everybody on the bus. It's only mid-morning but already he's had a skinful. "Too many people 'assatrouble. Westafrica'neastafrica'ntha. Six families tae a hoose. The Ashian shituashion. I know, I know." The other passengers seem to find him funny. He's a Scotch comedian pretending to be a drunk. They nod and smile and shake their heads to one another. Joan is alone.

Then one night, with winter coming on, she gets on the bus to come home and as soon as she sits down at the back she knows she has done the wrong thing. There are three boys just in front of her—all these young lives seem to come in threes—and apart from them the lower deck is empty. They are busy carving up the seats. She should get up and move to the front but she doesn't want to draw attention to herself. She listens to the blades slicing through plastic. The bus stops and an Inspector gets on, a Sikh. "Oh, here we go," says one of the boys, "a fucking towelhead. Eh, lads, feet up on the fucking seats." Joan sits mesmerised. The Inspector is a middle-aged man with a full, greying beard. He comes down and checks their tickets, then hers. As he goes back past them he says, "Take your feet off the seats, please." He can't help but see the ripped covering. "Fuck off ya black cunt ye." He calmly walks to the front of the bus, where he speaks first to the driver, then into his radio. At the next stop the boys run off the bus.

Joan breathes out. The air is so oppressive. She just sat back, shrank back in her seat and hoped it wouldn't touch her. She has to admit her fear.

It's not just that she is frightened about things like that. She thinks about what she is becoming, has become. She keeps telling herself that she could be a lot worse off, that she and Dan have a roof over their heads and two jobs that are secure and a holiday every year (not that they go away, but the option is there) and all right it would be nice to have children but she doesn't really know if it would be, she just says that because it's expected of her, not that anyone ever says, "Wouldn't you like children?", she wouldn't think much of someone who came out and asked as personal a question as that, not after all this time. But she can't avoid the truth. She can cope with her own life now simply because, at some point, she can't remember when, she lost the courage to change. It's not that she doesn't have fear—she has. It's that she doesn't have courage.

And what would her children be? Like those boys, those girls? It's too late, but she can't help wondering.

Yvonne says to Dan, "You've got to put your foot down. Brian abuses you, Diane exploits you. You're exploited. I mean, we all are, but we get paid enough for it. You do far more than you need to for them. Coming in at the weekend last week. Staying on to change her office around for her. They don't even thank you for it. You're a really nice man, everybody likes you, we only want to see you getting fairly treated."

"I'm all right," he tells her. "I appreciate your concern, but really I'm all right. I'm quite happy doing that kind of thing."

Although they don't own a car Dan and Joan have a problem with car ownership. Many of the neighbours who have cars have had them fitted with alarms, and the alarms keep going off, usually at two in the morning. Dan hates them. "It's just blatant selfishness," he rants. "Every time they go off they're saying, I'm looking after Number One, don't touch, I've commandeered the space in and around this tin box and if the wind buffets it or someone knocks it trying to squeeze by to get to the pavement and your sleep's disturbed that's tough, that's not my problem." Joan says: "They have to protect their property. I know what you mean, but they have to do something." "They're noise pollutants," says Dan. "Those alarms going off is a worse kind of pollution than the exhaust fumes." One night Dan's going to sort them. He'll go down into the street in his pyjamas and take a hammer to the windscreen of the screaming car, and for good measure he'll smash in the headlights flashing in time with the alarm. "Now you've something to make a fucking noise about," he'll shout. And all the people leaning out of their windows in their nightwear, the non-carred, cheering and applauding.

Joan at work. One of the salesmen is called Maurice. The first thing to notice about Maurice is his hair. It stands upright and waves like a cornfield in the breeze. It does this by design not by nature. He keeps it corn-coloured too and it looks absurd on a fifty-year-old. Margaret, who works with Joan, christened him The Coxcomb, and they all take the piss out of him, but Maurice is immune to anything that might alter his own good opinion of himself. If you're on your knees in front of the filing cabinet Maurice is the guy that always says, "Say one for me when you're down there, love." Or if you're not wearing your best smile he'll say, "Cheer up, it might never happen." At quiet moments he deigns to lean on their counter, practising his chat-up lines. As soon as a customer appears he skates off again: "A woman's work is never done, isn't that right, Joan?" "It's well seen a man's work never gets started in here," says Margaret. But Maurice can make a sale in twenty minutes and float back with his ego refuelled. An Asian man approaches the desk. "Oh-oh," says Maurice under his breath, "looks like you'll be trading on the black market this afternoon, ladies." "What was that, Maurice? I didn't quite catch that," Margaret calls after him, but Maurice is back among the new cars, on his own territory.

The women are talking about *Thelma and Louise* one day. It's not long out on video. Margaret's saying, "It's brilliant, the way she lets that bastard have it," and suddenly Maurice is there, sidling in.

"Is that the film about the two lezzies?"

"No, Maurice, it's not," says Margaret.

"Only joking," he says, "I saw it myself. Liked the music."

"Oh, just the music?"

"Well, some of the rest of it was a bit O.T.T. if you want my opinion."

"Did you not think he was asking for it, then?"

"Oh, now, I'm not saying he was right, of course I'm not. The guy was out of order, no question."

"He was raping her, for God's sake," says Margaret.

"Ay, but he backed off. I mean, she shot him after he'd backed off. A bit strong, surely."

"Sounds fair enough to me," says Joan. She's amazed at herself. She hasn't even seen the film.

"Joan, I'm disappointed in you," says Maurice. "I didn't think you were into women's lib. All these years we've worked together, Joan, and I never knew you were for burning your bra."

"You're pathetic," says Joan, "if that's what you think

women's lib is about. You're pathetic anyway." She can't believe she said that. Neither can Maurice. He retreats, pink-faced, the coxcomb bouncing ludicrously. Margaret hoots derisively at his back. "Imagine being married to it," she says.

And Joan feels good. She suddenly feels alive. She feels sorry about telling Dan to stop moping about with Billie Holiday. She wants to speak to him, to tell him that they do know what love is, they've just let it get buried somewhere along the way. As soon as she gets a quiet moment she's going to phone him, just to see if he's home, just to let him know she's thinking about him. All this distance they've let come between them, a lot of it's her fault, she wants to try and break it down. Maybe they could move away, start again somewhere where no one knows them. Maybe it's not yet too late.

Twice, sometimes three times a week, Dan has the flat to himself for a couple of hours. And one Saturday morning in three. These times are good for listening to records, reading the paper, watching something on the telly that Joan doesn't like or approve of. And sometimes they're good for other things.

Sometimes Dan gets out his magazines. The best bit about the magazines is after you buy them but before you start to read them. Even before you get home, walking back with them under your jacket, it's like you've bought an entry into another life. At this point they can contain anything, anything you want them to. The perfect woman might be in there, the woman that's perfect for you. It's only once you read them that the disappointment sets back in. You're always disappointed. The other life never lives up to your expectations. This is the nature of the magazines, their purpose, to leave you dissatisfied and send you back, sooner or later, for more. Dan understands this, but it doesn't stop him doing it.

Lately some of the magazines have started advertising phone-lines. Lately Dan has started reaching for the phone. It's a new thrill, he knows it won't last for ever. But just for now he likes what he hears, the security of the women's voices, the repetition of familiar phrases. He likes the posh voices that say, you can suck my nipples, and the taunting voices that say, get down on your knees and beg for it, but most of all he likes the close, breathy voice that says, I'm glad you're here and we're all alone. . . . It's pathetic really, he knows what a con it is. Maybe it's this, and not the loneliness in the woman's voice, that sometimes brings the tears after he has come.

All Dan wants is something else, for life to be something more than what it is. He is a nice man, a decent man. Really he is. But when he looks in the bathroom mirror, cleaning up, he does not much like what he sees.

Joan has a breathing-space, a lull. No phones ringing, nobody returning their car. Outside, the air thickens. She dials the number. In the space before the connection is made, she wonders if he'll answer, if he got home before the snow. She hopes so. She hopes he is safe. She wants everything to be all right.

Portugal 5, Scotland 0

On the one hand, I was saying to Bill, so much has happened. After MacDiarmid, and the great shift in people's attitudes to Scottish literature, culture, language, identity—things are so much more positive. I'm speaking for myself, maybe, but I feel optimistic, in spite of the politics, in spite of everything. Think of how different we are from twenty years ago. Scotland, I mean. Nobody can put that clock back.

On the other hand, of course, we were kissing America '94 goodbye. Bill and I had come in at half-time, to find us two-nothing down. Well, that was it all over really. Maybe that's why we moved on to talk about poetry.

The odd thing was, the rest of the guys in the bar didn't seem too upset about the football. The place wasn't that crowded, which may have had something to do with it, there wasn't that feeling of total anguish and despair. They weren't distraught in the way that they would have been ecstatic if it had been Scotland putting the goals away. Maybe nothing surprises any of us any more. Maybe we've all been hit so many times in recent years that a beating like that simply felt natural. To be honest, it was such a disaster you just had to put it behind you.

Mightn't do any harm, a spell of reassessment, I remember saying, as Barros slammed another one home. Rebuild the team, take a good long hard look at ourselves. And we turned away from the screen because it was distracting us from the literary questions in hand.

Not that the others in the bar were bothered about poetry, but—maybe it was just my mood—they didn't seem that far away from it. It was as if all of us in there, whatever we were talking about, had suddenly got beyond the football.

I'm hopeful, I said, just about the time Cadete got the fifth. We don't need a huge thistle-like figure always at our head, always to look to for guidance. What's done is done. He changed everything, and you have to be grateful for that. But the world's changed too. He was of his time, it's his poetry that transcends. I'm very hopeful. You have to be. First the culture shifts, then everything else. It's unstoppable.

I'm happy to go along with that, said Bill. Actually, I'm not representing him fairly at all. He'd done his share of the talking. It's just that we seemed to agree about most things.

The final whistle blew. It meant we could face the other way again.

Tilt

"What's it about? That's the only question in the world worth asking."

"What do you mean, what's it all about?"

"Not *all*. Just what's it about. What's it all about's a different question and it's too big."

"All right. What's it about. What do you mean anyway, ya picky bastard?"

"Well, like you're in a museum, or a gallery say, looking at a painting, and you ask, what's it about? Or you read a book, or you go to the pictures, or you see something on the news, or a fight in the pub. Or a woman crying in the street. Anything. What's it about?"

"Probably it's not any of your business."

"You can still ask it though. Into yourself like."

"Then you wouldn't get an answer."

"You might. You've only got to ask the question and find out. But all right, so maybe you don't get an answer. You still asked the question. You can come back to it another time. If it's important you *will* come back to it."

"You might think you've got an answer but it's the wrong one."

"It doesn't matter. You've still got an answer. I'm not saying it has to be right. You just have an explanation. Maybe the next time you come back to the gallery and go to that painting, you'll think, ah, *that's* what it's about. All right, so you were wrong before. It was still the only question worth asking. And anyway the answer can change. The answer is fluid. Only the question is a certainty."

"I'll tell you what's a certainty. You talking a lot of bollocks, that's what."

"Thanks, neighbour. You want me to roll another one of these?"

There was a time when Alan was ten, or maybe twelve. And this was what he was thinking, that that time was two-thirds of his life away. Right enough there was a time when he was five that was even worse—six-sevenths of his life away—but you don't remember the very early years at all, not at all. And yet they're the ones that make you. You're made in just a few years, and then the rest is unmaking. Did he really believe that? It was just that sometimes it seemed everything you did was a response to conditions. You didn't make yourself but were made by others, by what happened to you in childhood, and then as an adult it was as if you could only behave the way you'd been designed, buttons were pressed and levers pulled and all you could do was react. Parts of his childhood he remembered with amazing clarity, feelings and smells that immediately transported him back, and yet it was so distant, it was like somebody else's life. A previous existence. The clock was ticking and back then he had been impatient with its slowness but not any longer. Now it went with a speed that was terrifying and there was a simple reason: he wasn't young any more.

But even then, at twelve years old, he was worrying about the big things. He used to lie awake at night, spinning in his bed, pondering the mysteries of the universe: he was in bed because it was night; it was night because the earth turned on its axis once every twenty-four hours, and during half of these hours the side of the earth with Scotland on it faced away from the sun; here it was dark, on the other side of the earth it was light. And the nights were long now because it was winter, and winter was because it took the earth three hundred and sixty-five and a quarter days to orbit the sun, and in the winter months Scotland was further away from the sun than in the summer, while in New Zealand—the *antipodes*, meaning "diametrically opposite" although this wasn't really the case—it was summer at Christmas. The further north or south you went from the equator the colder it got because the poles were the points on

108

earth where the angles of the sun's rays were at their weakest. Scotland had a cool climate because it wasn't far from the arctic circle, northern Scotland was in fact on the same latitude as bits of southern Alaska. All this was disturbing; it meant, if it was true, that the tiniest shift could completely alter or even destroy the climate. He watched an old film called *The Day the Earth Caught Fire*, in which a series of nuclear test explosions knocked the earth off its axis, and worried about it for weeks afterwards.

The earth orbited the sun because of gravity, and the sun was a huge mass of blazing gases suspended in space, and the moon exercised its influence on the earth also, pulling the waters on the surface of the earth to and fro, creating the tides. And the sun was a star, and at night when Scotland had its back to the sun you could see hundreds of other suns, each of which might have their own system of planets, and the stars you could see in the northern hemisphere were different from the ones you could see in the southern hemisphere, it was like looking out of the front and back windows of a house, and the light from the stars took so long to reach earth that they might no longer be where they had been, they might have burnt out or exploded thousands of years before. And there might be life there too.

There might be life. That was an incredible thought, at once both exciting and frightening. He read *The War of the Worlds* and *The Day of the Triffids* and was invigorated with fear. He couldn't help himself. Only a year or two earlier he'd been reading all the Narnia books and believing in them. He actually believed them and that if he could only find the way in, through a wardrobe or a picture on the wall or whatever, he could get there too, to Narnia. Dangerous books to give to an imaginative child! Aslan, that bloody lion. He'd prayed to a bloody lion, for heaven's sake! Luckily he didn't tell anyone, and within two years just the unspoken memory was embarrassing. But even after he outgrew the lion he still believed that there might be life somewhere else.

And space went on forever, that too was a truly amazing thing, it made your head hurt trying to imagine what it meant, the implications of it. Infinity. At school he and his friends tried to write down infinity: a 1 followed by a pageful of zeros. Or it went like this:

Alan Sangster
31 Wallace Road
Burnside
Wherrieston
Stirlingshire
Scotland
Great Britain
United Kingdom
Europe
Eurasia
The World
The Solar System
The Universe

and some, under this, laid an 8 on its side. Smart-alecks, Alan thought. Their sickly 8 was no measurement of creation at all. Creation was a glass box containing the deep blue of space and all the planets and the sun and the other stars, with God outside holding the glass box, and to think of infinity you had to smash the box and obliterate the white-bearded image of God in an effort to conceive of something that never ever came to an end. It was like living in the fifteenth century and believing the earth was flat, and sailing in a tiny wooden ship to find the roaring cataract that was the edge of the world and never finding it, *proving yourself wrong*, sailing ever onward while your confidence grew and your fear of a quickening current diminished, on and on until you began to doubt your new belief that the world must in fact be round, and then, as the awful truth of infinity grasped you, the fear came again, bigger, bigger than any human could cope with. Then you would believe in God again, because nothing else could explain it. Because, if the universe was constantly expanding, if there was no glass box holding it all together, where was it expanding to? If everything was flowing ever outwards, away, all matter disintegrating in a mad chaotic rush, how long before the earth and Scotland and he in his bed got caught up in the flood and then what? No, no, it was impossible to understand the enormity of it. His head would explode.

He wasn't young any more. It didn't matter what the old folks said. His grandad and his uncles said he had his whole life ahead of him. If he was unhappy, well—he could always change his job, take up new interests. He was still young enough to start again. But how could you? Starting again was like unmaking, not possible. It was fine for them to talk, the old buggers, going on about their lives. They could justify themselves. Their lives had big things in them. There was a time when he used to scoff and yawn at them when they spoke about the past, especially about the wars, but not any longer. He'd never been in a war so he should just shut up and listen. What was more, he never would be in a war. He was too old for it. He didn't want to be in one, of course, but there was no denying it was something to have lived through—if you did live, that is. It would shape you. Supposing instead of when he was at the university he'd been fighting somewhere. His whole outlook on life would be bound to be different—wouldn't it? He could understand about people not forgetting, he could even understand about them not forgiving. It made his blood freeze over seeing those films of the death camps: what if he'd seen them with his own eyes; smelt them? His grandad had fought in the first war, the one that was supposed to end them all, and he didn't have a good word for the Germans still. You couldn't blame him. And Uncle Jimmy had been a P.O.W. in a Japanese camp. He never spoke about it but you knew it was there in him. Maybe his grandad would have got over it but then the second war came along and confirmed all his views on the Germans. Once the name P.G. Wodehouse cropped up—they were doing some of his stories on the telly. That bloody traitor, said his grandad. He had nothing more to add on the subject. He used to like his books but he'd never read one since he made those broadcasts. It was like— what?—Alan saying he wasn't going to read Jeffrey Archer because he was a Tory. Well, it was true, he never was going to

111

read Jeffrey Archer though more because he was a wanker than because he was a Tory but there was no comparison really. You had grudges but in these times they tended just to fade away. You didn't nurse them. But his uncle now, being in one of those camps, that wouldn't fade away, it would always be with you, you'd carry something like that around inside you your whole life. Like if you were an American who fought in Vietnam. Or a Vietnamese who fought in Vietnam—funny how they always got forgotten, poor bastards, it was their country, they'd had it a lot bloody tougher than the Yanks. Or if you were sexually abused. Raped. How would you ever get over something like that? You wouldn't. You'd just carry it. It would be part of you, for good or ill.

He made it through school and then he was no longer a child. But neither was he the person he would become, he knew that in retrospect. The mysteries of the universe still interested him. Sometimes he would discuss them with the friends he had in those days. They were all students. There were one or two among them for whom there was no mystery: the same ones that at school had wrapped it all up with a symbol. For them, everything was explicable in terms of relativity, everything was physics and chemistry, maths and matter. Alan had lost touch with these guys—they always were guys—through a lack of mutual interest. It wasn't that he didn't like them at the time, he simply didn't believe them. They were only twenty or so, like the rest, they were just starting out too, and he didn't believe that they knew all the answers. Still, he enjoyed their company, listening to them dismissing God and telling everybody else how simple the universe really was, especially—and this was usually how these conversations got started—if there was a joint or two going round. If you had a head full of hashish then it almost seemed as though you could make sense of it all. And, yes, there might even be another universe on your very own thumbnail.

Gradually he came down to earth. Specifically, he grew more and more concerned with life on earth, those closer-to-home mysteries. He loved the idea of animals and birds and fishes and plants. They were real things but it was the idea of them he loved, the fact that they existed as much as the existence itself. He loved trees and walking among them, touching their bark and trying to reach around their trunks, or just imagining doing so. Because you didn't want people to see you at it. The minds of most people weren't open to the idea of things, only to the things themselves. If they saw you hugging a tree or even just thought you were contemplating doing it they'd have you marked down as a hippy or a loony and that wasn't it. He was profoundly ignorant about nature, but he loved the idea of the hare changing its coat in winter, of the snake shedding its skin, of the salmon's return to the place of its own spawning. He loved the turning of the seasons, of hidden crocus bulbs pushing their flowers up to mark the start of spring, of an entire wood shedding its leaves in autumn, of whole lochs and burns freezing over. When he bought his flat with the small, shared garden he put up a bird-table so that he could watch the blue-tits and sparrows squabbling over the food. One early evening in winter he saw a fox cross the garden, beautiful and glowing in the snow, and in the morning he found that the snow had melted and then frozen again where its paws had left their tracks. It was as if it had walked across Alan's memory, leaving its presence there indelibly. He felt privileged.

He led a quiet life. After university they all went their own ways and his was solitary. He had been a quiet one from the start really. There were worlds going on in his head and that seemed enough. Ten years on the only fellow-student he was still friendly with was Mike, and although Mike had discussed space with the others he wasn't like them at all. He wasn't one of the know-alls, he was better than that, he was a know-nothing. He believed that the fact of his being alive was utterly insignificant when measured against what he understood of time and space and energy, and that therefore he should adopt a suitably humble attitude to his environment. This caused him to drop out of his engineering course in the third year. He decided there were

113

enough machines around already, and engineers like himself should show some respect for the planet in their profession. It was better to repair than to create, he said. Ever since dropping out that was what he did, repaired things for people—cars, washing-machines, lawnmowers, power-tools. He took cash in hand and did enough work to satisfy his needs, which were few: home-brewed beer and an assortment of other more or less harmless drugs, some books, a guitar, jeans, a motorbike. He got semi-seriously into New Age philosophy and he told Alan he was settled for life. His motorbike was only a Honda 125 and when he rode it he wore an old denim jacket because he couldn't afford the leathers but he said he was happy. Alan was envious, although he was earning a lot more than Mike's uncertain income. They used to talk about these things over many beers in the pub or—more often—out at Mike's. They were still serious about the universe but they were getting down to particulars. Life's a doughnut, Mike said one time (he was halfway through a joint admittedly): you, he said, are living in the middle of the doughnut because you think that's where the jam is, whereas I am living on the edge. Where the sugar is, said Alan. Where I *know* the sugar is, said Mike.

One Saturday in April Alan went to the edge, to visit Mike. He hadn't planned to. He drove his compact and efficient second-hand Vauxhall Nova away from the shopping-centre, through the town, over the railway tracks and out past the industrial estate (where he worked through the week as a product-control manager in a packaging factory), and turned into the straggling scheme where Mike lived with his dad. Theirs was the last house on the scheme, hard up against a dull red wooden fence on the other side of which was a muddy field. There was a big sign up in the field and a bulldozer had been at work there. This is not uncommon, Alan thought. This is what happens. You go to the edge and when you get there you find that Miller Homes are putting up sixteen houses to the acre just beyond it.

He'd phoned up half an hour earlier from a call-box in the

shopping-centre. His lip was swollen and his jaw was starting to ache.

"Can I come and see you, Mike?"

"Ay, just come out. What are you phoning for? You should just have come anyway."

"Oh, I wanted to make sure you were in."

"I'm always in, amn't I? My dad's away to the game. I'll get the kettle on. Mona's here by the way."

"Oh."

"That's all right, isn't it?"

"Ay, great. Thing is, Mike, I'm in a bit of a state. I've just been in a fight."

"Fuck's sake. It's three o' clock in the afternoon. What happened?"

He'd gone into town, just for something to do. The pavements were thick with shoppers, even though it was sunny and dry and you'd think anyone with an ounce of sense would be getting out in the open. He didn't know why he was there himself. He saw the crowds of women and their men, and the bored wee kids, and the roving gangs of bored big kids, and he understood that most of them probably didn't know why they were there either. A nation of shoppers. He wandered around looking at CDs and books and sound systems, at clothes and labour-saving devices for the home, and even at sporting equipment. What on earth was he expecting to find in it all, some kind of revelation about himself? Maybe if he had a wife, or a girlfriend. But that wasn't it. There was something about everything that alienated him. His work, well, that was fair enough, everybody felt alienated from their work, the nature of the system did that. But he seemed to be cut off from everything society had to offer, and from most of the people as well. He tried asking himself Mike's question—what's it about, what's it about?—but it wasn't working, he was getting no reply. He suspected that this was because he couldn't help slipping an "all" between the "it" and the "about", even though Mike had told him not to. The only things that appealed to him were wild things—animals, nature, the stars—but he couldn't touch them, he couldn't make them a part of himself, or himself a part of them. It wasn't human to do that. Or was it? He hadn't a clue. He hadn't a clue about anything. He was even alienated from his flat, for God's sake. His new flat that was supposed to be home—he didn't want to be in it.

He found himself on a narrow street behind the centre, lingering outside a door through which he could see a long, low-ceilinged room stretching back, all ablaze with lights and loud with bells and buzzers. A sign above the entrance announced "AMUSEMENTS". It was years since he'd been in one of these places. He'd played a bit of pinball in the student union, but hardly ever since then. He stepped inside.

It was important not to be caught watching the people at the bandits and other games. Although there were quite a few folk scattered through the rows of machines there was no sense of a crowd, only of individuals grimly entertaining themselves. People became very defensive in here. They wanted to be left alone. They grew protective of the fruit-machine they were playing. If they saw you watching them at *their* machine they feared you were waiting till they ran out of cash so that you could move in and clean up with a single coin. They suspected you of an intimate knowledge of their favourite machine and it made them jealous. People snarled and snapped at each other. Sometimes there was a scuffle.

He went to the booth where a fat, balding man changed his five-pound note for coins. He wasn't interested in gambling, he wanted to play pinball, try out his skills, see if he could still rack up a few replays. But the pinball-machines were different from when he had last played. They were all electronic, with impossible targets and too much fancy gadgetry. He tried a couple but it seemed the machines controlled your play rather than the other way round. He scored ridiculously low scores.

He wandered down the aisles, dismissing the monster-zapping and the motor-racing and the missile-launching as childish and humiliating. He caught sight of himself in a mirror on a pillar and realised how awkward he looked. Anyone who thought being in this place was humiliating didn't have the right attitude to it. They should just leave. But he didn't. He was looking for something to relate to.

Then, towards the very back of the arcade, he saw a doorway leading to a smaller room. It was quiet and completely empty, and the reason was obvious: it contained six aged pinball-machines, the old mechanical kind. They were beautiful, if a bit battered, real pieces of art, but boring compared with the technology out the front. They were exactly what he was wanting. He could deal with them.

He checked each one in turn, familiarising himself with the points systems, the targets, the bonuses, how to trigger replays. He noted the images and the names: "JOKER POKER", "GUNSLINGER", "STARSHOOTER", "MATA HARI", "BILLION DOLLAR BASH", "BABE RUTH". He settled for "JOKER POKER" because he recognised it from his student days. He knew he could beat it.

He played two or three games without success, but at first this didn't matter. He was just getting back into it. The same movements, the same holding and releasing of the flippers, the same thrill of shooting a ball back up an alley it had just descended. But no two machines are identical, he should have remembered that, not even when they're the same game. This one was very sensitive. It reacted to the slightest nudge or knock. In the old days he'd been able to move the whole machine without getting a tilt, but not this one. Even if he hit the flipper a little too hard the lights went down and he lost the score for that ball. It began to irritate him.

He moved on to "GUNSLINGER" to see if that was any better. It was more complicated, though, and he would have to spend a lot of time on it to get a half-decent score. It was "JOKER POKER" he wanted to master again, but the machine wouldn't let him. The bastards who ran the place had set it wrong. He'd just be holding the ball with the left flipper, and letting it run with a wee jump over to the right flipper, and the machine would go fucking dead on him. He looked under it to make sure it was fully plugged in. It was. He simply wasn't being allowed to play it properly.

He'd paid good money and he wasn't being allowed to play. It was fucking crap. The third ball died on him only 200 points short of a replay and he swore at the machine and gave it a good kicking, stubbing his toe in the process.

A big guy in a tee-shirt that said "AMUSEMENTS" walked through the door from the front and came up to him.

"Who d'you think you are, Roger fucking Daltrey?"

"It's set wrong," said Alan.

"It's set fine," said the guy. "You're supposed to play it with your hands, not your boots."

"Don't fucking get on at me," said Alan. "You just have to touch the machine and it tilts, you should get it fucking sorted."

"I'll fucking sort you if you don't get the fuck out of here," said the guy.

"It's your fucking machines, man, they're all fucked," Alan shouted.

The guy belted him in the mouth. Before he could hit back Alan found himself being bundled out past the fancy machines in the front, another guy coming to help and sticking a couple of punches on his kidneys to prevent any retaliation. Through the mist Alan saw a man half-turning to watch him go, but the rest kept their eyes trained on the screens and dials in front of them. In a moment he was lying on the pavement, gasping for breath and tasting the blood in his mouth.

The guy in the "AMUSEMENTS" tee-shirt stared down at him. "If you've got a problem, pal," he said, "don't bring it in here, okay?"

"Just come over," said Mike. "Mona's a nurse, remember? She has to deal with the likes of you every weekend in casualty." He laughed. "Well, every weekend she's on. The one weekend she's not you turn up to keep her hand in."

Mike was out in the garage when he arrived, working on an enormous engine that looked as though it could have come out of the builders' bulldozer over the fence. Alan had a swollen mouth, aching back and sore foot, and as he brought the car to a halt he wondered about himself again. What was he doing, disturbing Mike on a Saturday afternoon just because he'd got a beating he'd asked for? All over the country the other young men were well occupied: Mike was sorting something broken and he probably wasn't the exception Alan thought he was; others were at the football (including Mike's dad, and he wasn't even a young man), watching it or playing it, or waiting for the results to come up on the television; others were climbing mountains, painting houses, washing cars, building boats, looking after the kids, fishing, walking the dog, shopping even. Not Alan. He was keeping Mike from his work and looking for something. Company, answers, a laugh, a plan for the night. He was bored and lonely. He was looking for answers.

Mona was Mike's sister. She didn't live at home any more, she was just back from Glasgow for the weekend. She cleaned up his face while Mike made the tea. How useful they all were, these people. Here was Mike making things work so they wouldn't be thrown away, and his sister making people work so they wouldn't be thrown away, and their dad used to be a miner till British Coal threw away the pit, and their mum had been a gem, producing and nurturing this really useful family (until she died because she wouldn't stop smoking)—and then there was Alan! Not for the first time he felt inadequate. And it wasn't just the incident in the amusements place. That was nothing. It was everything else—his job, his house, his life, everything. Packaging was a *bad* scene. It was not environmentally a friendly way to behave, not with the packaging his company produced—full of CFCs and other time-bombs. I am not a useful person at this moment, he thought. I am out of kilter with the scheme of things.

Mike went back out to the garage after he'd heard about the fight—he had a good laugh about it—but Alan stayed for another cup with Mona. They'd met once before at somebody's wedding and she'd seemed all right but she was with some guy with sculptured features who didn't like her talking to other guys so they'd not had a chance to speak.

"What are you doing getting into fights?" she said. "You don't seem like—I mean, from what Mike's told me about you—you don't sound like that at all."

119

"I'm not," he said. "I don't know what got into me. I think I'm having some kind of crisis."

"What, about pinball?" she said.

"Ay, I'm hooked on it," he said. "I'm selling the furniture in the search for that elusive triple replay."

"So what's it about?"

"Christ, you sound just like your brother," he said. But she kept staring at him, expecting an answer.

"I don't know. I suppose I'm getting to that stage of wondering what I'm doing. I mean, I'm comfortably off, my job's pretty secure, but it doesn't seem good enough. I know, I know, that sounds like I've reached my thirties and can afford the luxury of gazing at my navel, but that's how I feel. The trouble is, it's not really anything new. I've been like this all my life. I'm the world's worst worrier, but not about wee things—about muckle great big things. Sometimes I wonder if I'm the next Messiah but somebody's forgotten to tell me. It's a cliché but there's got to be more to life than this."

"A relationship, maybe?" she said.

He shrugged. "I suppose it might take my mind off it." Then he asked her: "You still seeing that guy?" It might have been a leading question but it wasn't.

"Which guy?" she asked. Then she laughed. She knew fine. "No, he chucked me. I'm giving it a rest just now. It's hellish trying to have a serious relationship when you do the shifts I do."

"Well, have a non-serious one," he said. So maybe it had been a leading question after all. "With me."

She laughed again. "For a guy with a burst lip you're not backward in being forward anyway."

"Ay, well," he said, "don't mind me. But honestly, what do you think? I mean, what do you think it's about?"

"Your crisis, or life in general?" she asked. "Or can we apply the same question to both?"

"Ay, definitely," he said. "I think I'm having a crisis because I feel I should know by now what it's about. I mean, what are we here for, if not to know why? Or to wonder why? If we don't even wonder, what's the point of anything?"

"Oh, dear," she said. "What did you study at uni?"

"Business studies and management," he said. "Probably a mistake."

"Probably just as well. Imagine what you'd be like if you'd done metaphysics and moral philosophy." Mona reached behind where she was sitting on the floor, leaning against the sofa, and pulled a carrier bag towards her. She said, "I know just the thing for you. I was reading about it earlier. Pelmanism."

"Eh?"

She pulled out a handful of paperbacks from the bag. "I collect these," she said. "The old green-covered crime books. Penguins mostly, but also the Collins Crime Club ones, Crime Book Society—look." He flicked through them. 6d or 1/6 a time, they were mostly from the thirties and forties. Some of the earlier ones had the dustjackets still on them. "Do you read them all?" he asked.

"Oh, ay," she said, "I like a good thriller. But it's the editions really—they seem to be so much of a period. I don't go beyond 1960—well, you have to draw the line somewhere. Everybody seemed to do them in green until about then. And after that the jacket designs aren't uniform. I've picked up hundreds for virtually nothing. I just got these today—there's a secondhand bookshop up Spittal Street."

"I know where you are," he said. He looked again at the books. Rex Stout, Seldon Truss, Hulbert Footner, Erle Stanley Gardner, John Dickson Carr. "Great names," he said.

"Anyway," she said, "the books are irrelevant to what I was going to say." She picked up *The Broken Vase* by Rex Stout and turned to the inside front cover. "'The Grasshopper Mind'," she read.

"What's that?"

"'You know the man with a "Grasshopper Mind" as well as you know yourself. His mind nibbles at everything and masters nothing.'" She broke off. "This is an advert, not the plot. Isn't it great? Do you recognise yourself? I tell you, I'm convinced and I've not even got to the bit where you send off for further details.

121

"'At home in the evening he tunes in the wireless—tires of it—then glances through a magazine—can't get interested. Finally, unable to concentrate on anything, he either goes to the pictures or falls asleep in his chair. At his work he always takes up the easiest job first, puts it down when it gets hard, and starts something else. Jumps from one thing to another all the time.

"'There are thousands of these people with "Grasshopper Minds" in the world. In fact they are the very people who do the world's most tiresome tasks—and get but a pittance for their work. They do the world's clerical work, and the routine drudgery. Day after day, year after year—endlessly—they hang on to the jobs that are smallest-salaried, longest-houred, least interesting, and poorest-futured!'"

"Now you're talking," he said.

"Me more than you," she said. "I'm a nurse, remember?"

He put his hand to his jaw. "How could I forget?"

"'What Is Holding You Back?'" she said. "'If you have a "Grasshopper Mind" you know that this is true. And you know why it is true. Even the blazing sun can't burn a hole in a piece of tissue paper unless its rays are focused and concentrated on one spot! A mind that balks at sticking to one thing for more than a few minutes surely cannot be depended on to get you anywhere in your years of life!'"

"This is depressing," he said.

"It's all right," she said, "it gets better. 'The tragedy of it all is this: you know that you have within you the intelligence, the earnestness, and the ability that can take you right to the high place you want to reach in life! What is wrong? What is holding you back? Just one fact—one scientific fact! That is all. Because, as Science says'—that's Science with a capital 'S' by the way—'you are using only one-tenth of your real brain-power!'"

"If that, this afternoon at any rate," he said.

"'What Can You Do About It?'" she demanded. "You're not going to believe this."

"What?"

"'Take up Pelmanism now!'"

"The card game?"

122

"No," she said, "though I think this must be where the name came from. Something called the Pelman Institute, Norfolk Mansions, Wigmore Steet, London. Established over fifty years, callers welcome. 'A course of Pelmanism brings out the mind's latent powers and develops them to the highest point of efficiency. It banishes Mind wandering, Inferiority, and Indecision, and in their place develops Optimism, Concentration, and Reliability, all qualities of the utmost value in any walk of life.'" She closed the book. "Alan, this is for you. God, that was as good as a novel itself."

"It's uncanny," he said. "You hardly know me, nurse, and yet you've described me to the very roots of my being. Are you some kind of witch?"

"That's what my dad thinks. He thinks Mike and me are both witches because we're into things like aromatherapy and yoga and meditation."

"What about astrology?" Alan asked. "Or tarot?"

"Naw," she said, "that's all shite. I'm a practical down-to-earth kind of witch."

"Well, that's reassuring," he said. He picked up the book and looked at the ad. He turned to the inside back cover. "Hmm, I think I prefer the other solution to life's problems: 'Chocolate, chocolate, chocolate, chocolate, chocolate—I WANT CADBURY'S!'"

"That's just a temporary fix," she said. "I think we should try this Pelmanism thing out."

"Och," he said, "even if they're still going they'll not still be at that address."

"I don't mean that," she said. "I think we should have a *game* of Pelmanism. Sharpen your senses up a bit."

"All right." She had a very persuasive manner. He was forgetting she was Mike's sister and thinking of her more as a nurse skilled in the ways of the black arts, which was an appealing combination.

Mona stood up and fetched a pack of playing-cards from a drawer. She shuffled them, then laid them out on the floor face down in eight rows of six and one row of four.

"I haven't done this for years," she said. "Do you know how to play?"

"Ay, it's just memory, isn't it? Collecting the cards in pairs?"

"Well, you start then," she said. "Your need's greater than mine."

"I don't really see how this is going to help," he said. But he picked up a card from the top row, then one from the bottom. The ten of diamonds and the ten of spades.

"Wow!" he said. "Do they have to be the same colour?"

"No, not this time," she said. "Any pair will do."

He wasn't so lucky with his second shot. Mona had her turn without success. That meant there were four cards to remember. They both began to concentrate.

The door opened and a grey-haired man in a camouflage jacket came in.

"Hello, Alan. Been in a fight, Mike's telling me."

"Hello, Mr Aitken. Ay, nothing serious but. How was the football?"

"Ach, terrible! Two-nothing. That's them back down to the Second Division next season. I don't know why I bother going."

"Because you enjoy it," said Mona.

"Must be a masochist then," said Mr Aitken. "Anyway, looks like I'm interrupting. Anyone wanting a cup of tea."

"No, thanks," said Alan. "I've tea coming out my lugs."

"Right you are. Mona?"

"Not for me. Right, Alan. On you go."

"Wait a minute," he said. "Can we start this again?"

"How?"

"Well, we ought to be doing it right. Matching the colours, I mean—hearts with diamonds, spades with clubs."

"If you want," she said. "You feeling lucky?"

"I'm feeling something," he said. It was true. Something was building up in him. Maybe it was the house—Mike and Mona and their dad—it felt very good. He thought of his work, and how he had to get out of it. His heartbeat quickened.

Mona swept up the cards, shuffled them again, and laid them out.

"Right," she said. "Strictly by colour."

Mr Aitken came back in with a cup of tea and sat down in an armchair. "Is it going to bother you if I put the results on?"

"Course not," said Mona. "Alan's staying for his tea, if that's okay." She smiled across at him.

"Fine," said Mr Aitken. "What are you two up to anyway?"

"We're sorting out the universe," Alan explained.

"We're sorting out Alan," said Mona.

"You want to watch her," said Mr Aitken. "She's a witch."

The results were being read out on the television. The volume was down low, and there was something very soothing about the rise and fall of the familiar voice, down for a home win, slightly up for an away win, level but up for a no-score draw, up on both sides for a score-draw. Alan felt himself slipping into it, even though he wasn't taking in the actual information. He began to turn up cards to the rhythm of the voice.

After about half a minute he heard Mona say quietly, "Dad, take a look at this."

He was turning them up now, one after the other, his hand moving across the spread of cards smoothly and easily. It was as if his hand knew which card to go for. His mind watched his hand doing it with amazement, then with growing confidence. Suddenly he knew he was going to do the whole lot in a oner.

He was aware that Mr Aitken had turned in his chair and was watching what was happening. Mona was resting back on her heels, one hand held to her mouth as if she was frightened to breathe. All that was needed was for Mike to come in and see it. But he couldn't stop now, he couldn't wait for Mike. There were the three of them in the room, all concentrating on the cards on the carpet, all watching his hand glide across them, turning up the two red queens, the two black fours, the two black aces, putting them to one side, going back for the next pair, on and on without hesitation, so that soon there were only a dozen cards left. And he knew it was going to be all right, that nothing could stop him now, that he would go on turning up the pairs and never make a mistake, not one, until he could pause, with only one pair left face downward on the floor, and look at them

125

both, Mona and her dad, and they could all breathe again, knowing that the last two had to match, they had to, and nothing could possibly come between him and them, no matter how long he waited.

Surprise Surprise

I'm out for a drink with my mate Donnie, and Donnie's telling me this story about how he's out for a drink on his own one Friday night and he's in some bar and there's some lassies there he kens, so he says to them where's the action the night then, and they joke with him, one of them says not with you anyway, but friendly like, till another one says, the one he really fancies actually, she says there's this party we're going to but you have to take a carry-out, you'll not get in without one. That's no problem says Donnie and he goes up to buy them all a round, that's a pint of lager for him and a vodka and orange and a white wine and soda and a half-pint of lager for them and also he gets in a bottle of wine and a dozen cans of lager. Will this do for a password he says, coming back from the bar for the third and final time. Ay that'll do the trick says Susie giving him this big sexy smile, she's the one drinking the lager which was why he kind of tipped the balance of the carry-out in that direction. Thank God for that he says because that's me skint, where's this party then. It turns out it's at this guy's flat that's going out with the wee blonde one. This is quite good for Donnie, it'll break the women up when they get to the party probably, the only drawback being if Susie's going out with some other guy in the flat, or meeting a guy there, or just doesn't fancy him, Donnie, at all, although he thinks she does, that way you get an instinct, a knowledge that it's going to be all right, the pair of you are going to end up together, which is a more exciting, more brilliant feeling somehow than the actual getting off itself. The third lassie, Lorna, she's talking about meeting HER boyfriend there, and dropping big hints like maybe this'll be your lucky night Susie and Susie going eh, oh shut up Lorna, but giving him wee funny smiles too. Ay, you ken somehow, Donnie says to me, when it's going to be all right.

Well, they leave the pub a while later and it's a cold night going down the high street but anyway they arrive at the flat where the party is to be. The place is pretty stowed and right enough there's some big fucker on the door going hi Susie hi Lorna and giving the blonde one Michelle giving her a big kiss but at the same time checking the carry-outs. He's with us says Michelle but the bastard still makes sure Donnie's poke's got bevvy in it, as if he might be carrying fake cans or something for fuck's sake. They go into the kitchen and Donnie's thinking ahead already, he's thinking I'll stick a couple of these cans in the fridge for show but the rest of it's going into hiding, so he finds a nice wee cupboard by the sink and stashes his bevvy behind the washing-powder. Susie and he crack open a couple of cans and Lorna opens the wine. So what does that guy do when he's not frisking his guests Donnie asks, because he's already decided he doesn't like the bastard, and Lorna and Susie both start giggling and Susie checks Michelle's not around before she says ay right enough he's a bit of a wanker. He's a lorry-driver says Lorna, he does long-distance trips, a week on a week off ken, to Europe and that. Oh says Donnie long-distance trips eh, I've been on a few of those myself and I don't even drive. Very clever says Susie. Very stupid says Lorna. Ay well says Donnie and the conversation moves on to something else.

After a while Lorna's boyfriend turns up and they go through to the front room to dance. The music's really loud. It's some of that thumpy-thumpy tshky-tshky music, ken the kind of thing, fucking terrible, it just goes on and on and then there's a pause and the next one starts and it's exactly the same only this time it goes tshky-tshky thumpy-thumpy. That's terrible music says Donnie, you'll not catch me going in there. What sort of music do you like then says Susie, oh he says anything that's good ken, R.E.M., Simple Minds, that sort of thing, what about you. Ay she says, R.E.M., I like them. And the next thing they're kissing, it just kind of happens, one minute talking the next minute kissing, and suddenly the kitchen doesn't seem so full of folk any more, like they've all gone through to dance, maybe they're embarrassed by them getting stuck into each other but Donnie and Susie don't care, they're just kissing. After a while they come apart and think about it for a minute, then they kiss again, then they break for a drink. Well, says Donnie. Ay, says Susie. They laugh. What were we saying before. Who cares she says. Are you all right he asks her. Ay she says I'm fine honest I've just drunk too much. He holds her close for a minute and it's great and then about that time she says I'm going to be sick and he has to take her off to the bathroom which luckily doesn't have the usual ten-minute queue outside of it. You want me to come in he says but she shakes her head and goes in and locks the door and seconds later he can hear her throwing up in the bog.

While he's waiting for her he becomes aware that the big bastard whose flat it is is watching him standing outside the bathroom door. He doesn't seem to be enjoying his own party much, in fact you wonder why he's even bothering to have one since he'd be happier being a bouncer at a nightclub, at least he'd get paid for it and probably be able to beat a few folk up although maybe that comes later thinks Donnie, because the guy's certainly managing to make him feel uncomfortable. So he sidles off out of sight out of mind through the nearest door which is into the bedroom where people have been dumping their coats. So he's in there while Susie's through the wall getting it out of her system, giving it laldy down the great white telephone to God, and he goes over to this bookcase because that's what you do, when you're on your own in someone else's room and you see some books, well you go and check them out, and it's not considered rude or out of order although in the case of this lorry-driver bloke you never know, but as a rule it's okay, it's not like going through their drawers or reading their letters or something, it's like an accepted thing to do, to look at a person's books, that is assuming they've got some. Well anyway so there he is and he reaches out one particular book because for some reason the title catches his attention, as if he's heard of it or should have heard of it before, the book is called "The Stories of Raymond Gunn". So he takes this book and it's all different stories and the very first page he opens it at, where he starts reading, he's right in the middle of a story, and it's about HIM.

It's about him himself, my pal Donnie, meeting these women in a pub and going to a party with them. This is pretty damn weird he thinks maybe somebody's slipped something into my drink, you never know what some bastards'll do for a laugh these days. So he pinches himself and keeks in the mirror but he's still all there as far as he can tell although if you think about it a mirror can't really tell you that, if you're ALL there, I mean it's not three-dimensional, and anyway supposing you're not there when you stop looking, when you turn your back you vanish, or to put it another way where's your image when it's not in the mirror, which is a question on the same principle as when a tree falls in the middle of a forest does it make a noise. Anyway he thinks I'd better read on a bit, so he does, and what does he find but that he gets to the party and he gets off with this lassie called Susie who ends up really out of her skull and having to go off and lock herself in the bathroom to be sick. And it's even got all the phrases in it, all the things he's been saying, even what he's been THINKING, like that bit about the great white telephone, that's in there, it's all written like a thingmy, stream of consciousness, James Joyce, Faulkner kind of thing, difficult to read stuff so you don't know who's speaking/thinking from one moment to the next, Donnie or me or Raymond Gunn or Raymond Gunn's book or what, you don't know if you're in the book, or if you're not in the book but you're about to be, or if you're reading this and you're a character in a story reading about yourself, nothing's certain about anything. This is spooky, Donnie thinks, I'm not sure about this at all, I'm off out of here. But he slips the book into his jacket pocket—he's never taken his jacket off since they arrived, that way you sometimes don't if you're not sure how long you're going to stay—he puts the book in his pocket because he wants to know what happens next, and if it does will it be the same as in the book.

Donnie hears the bog flushing and water running next door which presumably means Susie's about to make her return to the land of the undead, so he leaves the bedroom and goes back to the bathroom door so it'll be to her as if he hasn't moved at all the whole time she was in there. Except of course the lorry-driver kens he's been in and out of the bedroom although now he's back where he is he couldn't actually prove it. Well, the only way he could prove it would be by frisking him and finding the book on him, but then Donnie thinks if things are following a pattern he'll know he's got the book anyway, if he's read the stories before, if they're already written, if that's his bedroom, his book, if he maybe is Raymond Gunn himself. . . . About this time Donnie thinks he's losing his mind and it's time to leave the party.

So when Susie comes out he says are you feeling all right now and she says yea but not great and he says look I'm going to head off do you want me to see you home and she says ay okay but I'm not in a fit state for fighting you off ken and he says no it's all right I just want to make sure you get home safely. Right she says I'll get my coat because she unlike Donnie did take hers off when they arrived. So off she goes to get her coat and Donnie hangs around near the door with the big man still checking him out. Donnie's thinking Christ if he frisks me I'm dead I've stolen his book so he decides to engage the cunt in friendly conversation to distract his attention. He goes eh, good party mate, sorry to be leaving so soon but, ken how it is, need to see Susie home she's not feeling that good. The guy just stares at him and grunts as if to say I don't think your intentions are entirely honourable pal, which at one level would be a pretty accurate assessment but at another is wrong as Donnie isn't wanting to force the issue with Susie, not tonight if she's not feeling up to it. Then Donnie says, will you say cheerio to Michelle and Lorna for us and the guy grunts again. Finally Donnie says

So you're a lorry-driver.

The guy says Ay.

Oh says Donnie, but it comes out as a kind of grunt too. That's about the sum total of the dialogue between them.

Coming out onto the street Donnie minds he's left eight unopened cans of Tennent's lager in the kitchen cupboard. Fuck fuck fuck well there's no going back for them, it was hard enough getting them in, he'd be taking his life in his hands trying to get them out. Susie's hanging on to his arm having some sort of relapse. Donnie asks her what was the guy's name anyway. She doesn't answer so in a fit of genius he looks at the nameplate and surprise surprise he sees Gunn so he says I thought you said he was a lorry-driver and she says he is and he says well he's written a book unless I'm much mistaken and she says so, what are you saying, you can't write books if you've got an HGV licence is that what you're saying, you've got to have a degree in English literature or something because if you are you're wrong you're just wrong and prejudiced. No he says, I'm not saying that, so he's Raymond Gunn is he, is that him Raymond Gunn the famous writer. She says now you're just being sarcastic, you must be jealous. Anyway it's a joke, of course that's not his real name. Ray Gunn. He writes Science Fiction. Haven't you heard of aliases she says nom-de-plumes PSEUDonyms she says. Ay I've heard of them he says I've heard of pseudonyms I've just never met one before that's all.

And all the time Donnie's speaking with her, he's got his hand in his pocket feeling the smooth cover of the book, the glossy cover and its edges and corners, he's running his fingers over it thinking about what he's going to read in it, what it's going to be like reading it over again, reading it all over just exactly as it happened. He's not interested in Susie at all, when they were kissing before he was getting a hard-on but now he just wants to get shot of her, in fact if he sees a taxi he's going to put her in it with whatever money he's got left and walk home on his own. That'll make it an expensive night, the carry-out not drunk the taxi not ridden in the condoms not used (oh ay, forgot to mention them) but it doesn't matter at all to Donnie because all he wants to do is get home and get into bed with this book, this is the thing he's most wanted to do ever in his life, it's as if he's about to discover something about it, about his life.

That's what it was like says Donnie that book was going to be like a secret passageway to somewhere, in fact he says to me I've got it here, clapping his jacket just below the ribs, I've got it here. It's amazing he says. You'll be amazed.

Republic of the Mind

He was beyond the politicians. Way beyond them. If they couldn't get their act together when it was so obvious, he wasn't wasting his time waiting for them. He was off already—gone. To the republic of the mind. That's where he was.

It wasn't Robert, however, but Kate who threw the bottle through the TV set on election night. The Stirling result was what did it.

"I don't believe it!" she screamed. "If they can't get it right *there*!" The opinion polls had been like huge signposts pointing at the one opposition candidate who could capture the seat, but the good folks of Stirling appeared not to have taken the hint. Kate launched the empty Frascati bottle at the smiling face of the Government Minister, and his expression—happy or smug, depending on one's political viewpoint—exploded from the tip of the nose outwards into nothing. Everybody else in the room stared in awe at the dead screen. It was the kind of thing they'd always wanted to do—to politicians, princes, weather forecasters, game show hosts, footballers, sitcom characters—but their anger had never quite overcome their reluctance to pay the price.

There were seven or eight of them, and they had come to celebrate. It was understood that, even should the Tories get back in overall, they would be annihilated in Scotland. This would force a constitutional crisis. But only a few hours had passed since the polls had closed and already Scotland was snatching ifs and buts from the jaws of certainty. Kate's act of frustration at least put an end to the agony of watching any more results. After another couple of drinks the TV began to look good—much better than it ever had done—and even the next day, clearing up the cans and plates and the powdered glass of the screen from the carpet, neither Robert nor Kate wanted to disturb the bottle. It was a monument to the moment when they

133

left the politicians behind; a regrettable but glorious moment to be forever relived. Every time they looked at the neck of the bottle sticking out of the hole they were reminded of the Minister's exploding face.

Kate was reading a passage in a history book about the execution of Mary Stewart. She had learned to think of her by that name, it made her more human somehow. Kate wasn't into royalty:

> Then her dressing of lawn falling off from her head, it appeared as grey as one of three score and ten years old, polled very short, her face in a moment by so much altered from the form she had when she was alive, as few could remember her by her dead face. Her lips stirred up and down for a quarter of an hour after her head was cut off.
> Then Mr Dean said with a loud voice, "So perish all the Queen's enemies. . . ."

It was a different world, of course it was. It was four centuries ago and these people were the most important people in the land. And yet that was all they were, just people. The game they played—treaties, alliances, invasions, marriages, plots, executions—was a game of chess with human beings for the pieces. Queens, castles, clerics and knights, and, somewhere else, in a separate world again, cities full of pawns, a countryside dotted with pawn peasants.

For some days after the election Kate went around the flat muttering: "Hopeless, hopeless. Guns and bombs, guns and bombs, that's all there is to it." But she'd already had her act of violence. And Robert, too, simply shook his head and headed off to the republic of the mind. The politicians could follow when they were ready. Robert was there, and Kate a lot of the time, and also many of their friends, although they didn't always know it.

Sometimes, before she got there herself, Kate would realise he was in the room but absent from it. If the telly hadn't had a bottle in its face they would have been watching the news, or some

134

other useless programme. As it was, they'd be sitting—reading, maybe—and his book would fall aside onto the arm of the chair. Then she'd see the change in his face.

"Is that you away again?"

"Ay." His voice sounded distant.

"Where is it you go to?"

"Och, just away. I just think what a waste of time it is, having to wait to be a normal country, having to waste all this energy identifying ourselves. So I bugger off anyway. To the Scottish republic of the mind."

She thought about that. It sounded not a bad idea at all.

"Oh, ay, what's it like there? Is it any better than the Scottish province of the body?" So Robert could tell she was probably almost there herself, coming out with a remark like that.

"Brilliant," he said. "It's brilliant."

It might have been a drug, it might have been something you scored in pub toilets, but it wasn't. It was better than that, and it didn't fuck you up either. It didn't make your nose cave in or give you monsters in the shadows or even just a rotten head, in fact it was an antidote to the post-election hangover. One day everybody was going to be there. The last folk off the last bus would be the political parties claiming they'd just wanted to make sure nobody got left behind.

It was more than some utopian fantasy about society. It filled the gap between actuality and possibilities of all kinds. Somebody once said that the art of life lay in recognising the luminous moment. Robert wasn't certain about what that meant, what that moment might be, but he had some ideas. Neil Gunn had this concept—the atom of delight—a state of contentment and completeness—"*I came upon myself sitting there.*" The republic was something like that, except it was constant, and for everybody. It was a state of being in which all the people understood themselves, and what they were doing, and why they were where they were. The more often you got there, the longer you stayed. And this was the secret of it—it didn't depend on the politicians at all. It didn't need constitutions and laws, but simple self-determination. It was as if every individual made their own Declaration of Arbroath. It was like going up to the mountain, and coming down whole.

Robert could remember with startling clarity the first real moment between him and Kate. This was a different kind, though, a moment shared between two people only. They'd known each other for months but up till then nothing had happened between them. Afterwards they discovered that they had each thought they were unnoticed by the other. They were in a crowd in some bar, surrounded by friends, and finding themselves pushed closer and somehow isolated from everybody else, they both became suddenly aware of their togetherness. It was as if all the people in the bar withdrew some distance, leaving them in a space of their own, although the fact was that the elbows and arms still jostled and squeezed around them. They kissed. Everybody might have been watching but they wouldn't have seen that kiss. It was beyond the din and heat of the bar. The kiss was loaded with possibilities. It was what had carried them forward to where they were now, two years later. They were still unwrapping the possibilities it had contained.

That was just one moment. It meant everything, Robert was certain—it and other moments that stood out of daily life like islands in a loch. How, if they meant less than everything, did they return over and over to him? He knew that in ten or twenty or thirty years they would still be as clear and miraculous as they were now, as they had been when they first took place. He gathered them like the jewels of life.

He understood that he had a religious frame of mind. He was not church-going, he was past that, although he didn't mock it as he once had. He was in his thirties and sometimes he thought he would like to go to church again, but it wasn't for him. On the odd occasions when he did enter a church—at weddings, at funerals—he sat upright and watched, and knew he wasn't a part of it. From his place in the pew he confronted the pulpit, the communion table. He was not being irreverent. It was a throwback, maybe, to his upbringing, to the Presbyterian in him, to a grim determination to meet God halfway, open-eyed, on equal terms.

And yet he was religious. Or, rather, he understood what religion was. He understood that its purpose was to explain. He knew he was a speck of dust, almost nothing, and yet he saw himself in relation to everything. He could be himself and yet be outwith himself. Christ was man and God. That was him too—dust and life, nothing and everything. There was something in that universal relationship that made him sick with excitement. He heard with awe the words of MacDiarmid echoing around the planets—awe both at the idea and at the mind that produced the image:

> I' mony an unco warl' the nicht
> The lift gaes black as pitch at noon,
> An' sideways on their chests the heids
> O' endless Christs roll doon.

He could see how a man like the ecologist John Muir could take the best from his father's harsh, rigid creed and turn it into a celebration of existence, a hymn of joy. He believed that Muir must have had these moments too. In fact, a man who would climb a tree in a storm, to see what it was like to be a tree in a storm, probably had them all the time.

Kate met him at the door of the flat one Tuesday evening. "Your mum phoned," she said. He knew at once that it was his father, that his father was dead. Kate hugged him. "I'm sorry," she said. "It was this afternoon. Your mum's just back from the hospital."

They'd been waiting for the phone-call for days. They'd been waiting for the days of waiting for months. Only two weeks ago they'd seen him, apparently recovering, but Robert knew, from what his dad had said before, that death wasn't far away. Just around the time of the election he'd been found to have cancer. He'd gone out to vote with a vengeance—"One last push for independence!" he joked, knowing that that wasn't going to happen but sure, like them, that something must give in Scotland. He didn't have the pleasure of seeing that, Robert thought. He went in and out of hospital, had days of slipping down and days of holding fast, then decided not to fight it any longer, that he wanted only to have some peace and to be free of pain. That was what he had told Robert. "It's time to go," he said. "Your mother doesn't think so because I'm only sixty-six, but it is." And now he was gone.

"Are you okay?" Kate asked him. She let go and stepped back. He nodded. "Ay, I'm fine. How's my mum?"

"She's all right, I think." He had sisters. They were with her. He picked up the phone and dialled, and spoke to them each in turn. The funeral was to be on the Friday. Robert would drive up there in the morning.

"Look," he said to Kate, "I'm all right, but would you mind holding the fort? Folk'll be phoning and I don't think I can handle it. I want to go out for a bit."

"Fine," she said. "Will you come back, or will I meet you?"

He thought of a quiet bar a couple of streets away. "Let's meet at the Ruthven. Say, in a couple of hours?"

He'd intended to go for a walk before having a drink—it was May, and the days were long and dry—but his way took him past the Ruthven anyway and he thought, to hell with it, I'll have several drinks. On my own. A wake without the body.

He'd cut back on the beer of late because he was getting a bit of a belly, but he wanted a long drink. A long drink and a short— a half and a half. He was thirty-one ordering an old man's tipple. He heard John Lee Hooker's raucous voice somewhere in his head belting out "One Bourbon, one Scotch, one beer". There were occasions, it seemed, when drinking was the best possible thing you could be doing.

There was an older man sitting next to him at the bar, a folded newspaper in front of him. They were both away with their thoughts. This was good: there was no necessity for small talk. But after about twenty minutes, when he was into the next set of drinks, the man said:

"I'll just say one thing, friend, and then I'll not bother you. Just one thing. See this privatising the water, it makes me boak.

It makes me want to join the tartan army or something."

Robert gave him a grin. "I know," he said. "They'd privatise the air if they could bottle it."

"That's all I wanted to say," said the man. "I'll not bother you any more."

"It's all right," said Robert. "I don't mind if you want to talk." It was true. He'd come in thinking he was going to do some thinking, but that wasn't how thinking happened. Not about your father who was dead. You had to come upon it, or it came upon you, more subtly than that.

The man was probably in his fifties. His jacket had seen better days. So had his trainers. His hair was thin and straggly and his face thin and tired-looking. But he had very bright blue eyes. They were what people would remember about him.

"The trouble is," he said, "we're powerless because there's too many issues. If water was the only thing on the agenda they wouldn't have a chance. Or if it was just about having our own parliament—if that was the only issue we'd have it by now. But it's not, we keep having to try to get Labour in down there as well, to, like, minimise the damage. Ken what I mean?"

"Ay," said Robert. He was thinking how nobody ever assumed their neighbour was a Tory in a public house in Scotland. "But self-government is the one unifying issue. If we had the parliament we could deal with all the other issues the way we wanted."

"Maybe, maybe," said the other guy. "But it's hard, isn't it? I keep thinking I'm going to stop doing it, vote Labour I mean, but then the next election comes along and there's all these other things you want to vote on. Don't get me wrong, I'm all for it— a Scottish parliament—but you can't isolate it like that. Sorry. 'Scuse me if you're SNP or anything."

"You've put it in a nutshell," said Robert. "And you're right. But self-government's the key, it's getting there that's the problem. I'm a tactician myself. I vote for whichever party's got the best chance of beating the Tory. Sooner or later we'll get what we want by default."

"So you'd not call yourself a nationalist?"

"My dad's a nationalist. That's as close as I get. He's on the thinking wing of the party, though, always has been. Understands what folk like yourself are saying. Me, I'm on the thinking wing of the people."

"Ay, right enough, most folk don't think much about it at all. And why should they? Seeing the politicians making such an arse of it."

"You're a man after my own heart," said Robert. To prove it, he bought the guy a drink. He was aware that his dad had come into the conversation. He should tell the guy he was dead. It didn't matter, but he should. He would, later.

"To be honest," he said, "after the last disaster, I've kind of given up on the political parties. I've kind of just gone ahead, myself and a few others. As far as possible I live life as if the republic's here already."

"That can't be very far," said the guy. "Or very possible. Bit of a pipedream that, I would say."

"Well, it is of course, but I don't see what else to do. I mean, if your mind's already arrived there, if you're psychologically and emotionally and culturally in that other place, it's just tearing yourself apart getting frustrated about the fact that the actuality is different. So, I know what you're saying, but it seems to me, if the attitude is there, the rest will follow."

The guy nodded. "I understand. But there's folk out there with fungus on the walls and no job and their benefit getting cut and fuck knows what else—I don't think your wee nirvana's going to help them much."

"Neither are the politicians. Politics has failed these people. Completely passed them by. They can forget about politics because the political system as presently constituted has forgotten about them. And maybe I am indulging in a bit of fantasy, but we can't all be Tommy Sheridan."

"He's as bad as the rest of them," said the guy.

"I'd have voted for him if I stayed in Pollok," said Robert. "At least he shakes the complacent bastards up a bit."

The guy bought them another round. Robert could understand why the auld fellows bought halfs and halfs. It got you

140

fucking steaming. No doubt he would pay for it the morrow though.

"Well, I'll tell you," said the guy, "this water thing, this is the last straw. They may not call it privatisation, but they'll try to sell it somehow, through the back door. I mean, how can you own it, for God's sake? It falls out the fucking sky!"

"'One does not sell the earth on which the people walk.' Crazy Horse said that. You know, Crazy Horse, Sioux chief?"

"One does not sell the water in which the fish swim. I said that. That's how poaching's all right by me—and everybody else I ken. You can't own the water so you can't own the fish that swim in it. Would you not say?"

"I would," said Robert. They drank to the fish that were nobody's, and pulled their stools closer. Robert got another round in.

At some point in the evening he looked at his watch. He had an idea that Kate was coming to meet him. He still hadn't managed to tell the guy about his father.

"One day," he said, "we'll get what we want."

"Ay, will we? I feel, personally, I feel time is passing us by. Suddenly you realise you're getting old and there's a chance you might not see it in your lifetime, ken?"

"See what?" Robert asked.

"Anything," said the guy. "See anything you want to see. I'm not talking just politics. I'm not meaning home rule or independence or whatever. I mean, bigger than that. Everybody should see something in their lifetime that they'll never ever forget. That they're a part of. That nobody can take away from them."

We're a nation of philosophers, Robert thought. That's what we are, at the end of the day. A nation of fucking philosophers.

"The big things in life," said the guy. "Life and death and that." And Robert remembered his father.

"I haven't told you," he said. "There's something I haven't told you."

"Me too," said the guy. His bright blue eyes were brighter still.

"It's about my dad," said Robert. "Mind I said about my dad

141

earlier, about him being a nationalist?"

"You're beautiful," said the guy.

"Eh?" said Robert. "No, about my dad."

"You're beautiful. I'll just say that. The most beautiful bloke I've ever seen."

"What?" The guy's blue eyes were full of tears.

"Do you want to come back with me?" he said. "Do you want to come back home with me?"

"Oh, God," said Robert. "Oh, God, I'm sorry, mate. I didn't even know what you were talking about. No, I'm sorry. I'm no that way, you know? I'm sorry."

The guy looked like he'd heard it before. His face, briefly animated, became tired again.

"That's all right," he said. "Sorry to bother you. Don't fucking, don't fucking hate me, eh?"

"Naw," said Robert. "Course not. Christ, we've just had this conversation. We agree about everything. I'm just not into it, that's all. You know, with another man. I'm sorry."

"I'm no a pouf," said the guy. "Folk always think you're a pouf. It's just how I am. I'm a human being." He made as if to move away.

"It's all right," Robert said. "I'm not offended. You don't have to go, for fuck's sake. Please don't feel you have to go."

He shook his head. He was such a fool sometimes. So blind not to see what the guy was wanting. And yet it wasn't just that. They'd had this long talk. They'd understood each other in other ways.

There was a hand on his shoulder, and he jumped. It was Kate's. "Sorry," she said. "I kept trying to come over but the phone kept ringing. Are you all right?"

"Ay. I'm pretty fou but. What time is it?"

"It's nearly ten. Have you been here all this time?"

"I skipped the walk. Listen, Kate, there's this guy I met. A really nice guy." But the man was gone. He must have slipped away when Kate appeared. Robert said:

"I was going to introduce you but I didn't know his name anyway."

142

Kate sat on the empty stool and got herself a drink. "Just one, I think," she said, "and then we'd better get you home. Are you all right?"

"Ay. I'm just pissed."

"You're in a state."

"No, I'm okay, honest. Kate." He put his hand to her face for a moment. "Kate, I really love you, you know that?"

"I know," she said. "I love you too. So tell me about this guy."

They got back into the flat and while the kettle was boiling for coffee he knocked over the milk carton.

"You *are* pissed," she said.

"Sorry."

"It's okay. I was late. Anyway, if you can't drink at a time like this. . . ."

They went through to the front room and sat down. They sipped their coffee for a minute. She was going to put a record on but decided it wasn't appropriate. She said:

"I mind one time last summer, you were out with Joe and Mark. I stayed in, went to bed early. When you got back, you were really bevvied, really stinking of it. Do you mind this?"

He nodded. She wasn't sure if he was listening, nor was she sure what she was going to tell him.

"You got into bed beside me and that was all right. But after a minute you touched me. I remember I turned my back on you and got as far away as I could." She stopped again. When she said it aloud it didn't sound very dramatic, not the big deal she had in her head. There must be something more, at the end of what she was saying, but she didn't know quite what. She thought she might be upsetting him. "Should I be telling you this now?"

"Ay, tell me." He smiled at her.

"It's just you'll not remember." In the morning, was what she meant.

"I think I was just trying my luck," he said.

"Well, you weren't getting anything that night, that's for sure." They both laughed. After a pause he said:

143

"I don't blame you for turning away. If that's what you're wondering."

"No," she said, "that's not it. I mean, it was just at the time. I was feeling pretty scunnered at you."

"Sorry."

"No, it's okay. I shouldn't have got so tensed up about it. I lay awake for ages while you started to snore. I was raging. Like you'd deliberately insulted me or something. Completely stupid."

"Sorry."

"Don't keep saying that. I'm more angry with myself than you, when I think about it now. I should have got up and read a book or something. Letting a wee thing like that get to me. It was as if I was some snooty old bag in my fifties."

"What are you trying to say?" he asked.

"It's just," she said, "whenever I think about that, it's very clear in my mind. Just a wee incident. But I always think, wouldn't it be terrible if I'd lost you then? If that had been the moment when I lost you?"

He looked at her, a worried look. "Have you lost me?"

She touched his hand across the table with hers. "Never. I know that now." Then she said:

"I'm really sorry about your dad. He was a lovely man."

He nodded. "He was. He was one of the good guys."

Robert went to bed. Kate sat for a few minutes, letting the day go out of her head. She liked to do this, to think through the day and let it go bit by bit. She went to the bookcase and picked out the book of Scottish history. She kept going back to it, to the famous passages, as if it were a Bible. Nearly always she went to the brief fame of Kate Douglas, who tried to save her king, James Stewart, first of that name, before his assassins had him cornered in the sewer and finished him with sixteen deadly wounds to the breast:

And in the menetyme, quhen thay wer slayand him, ane young maidyn, namit Kathren Douglas, quhilk wes eftir maryit upoun Alexander Lovell of Ballumby, steikit the dure; and because the greit bar was hid away be ane traitor of thair opinioun, scho schott hir arm into the place quhair the bar sould haif passit; and becaus scho was bot young, hir arm was sone brokkin all in sondre, and the dure dongin up by force, throw quhilk thay enterrit, and slew the King with mony terribill woundis.

"Scho schott hir arm into the place. . . ." Such simple, desperate courage. One moment in a woman's life, and down the centuries all that was left of her life was that moment. But what a moment! What it spoke of, and left unspoken!

She got into bed beside him. They lay side by side. Then they turned and kissed for a while.

"Do I stink of beer?" he asked. "Or the whisky?"

"It's fine," she said.

He felt her mouth moving down his chest, across his belly. Then her hot breath was on his balls and penis. She ran her tongue up and down it. He felt himself slipping in and out of her mouth.

It wasn't right, though. It was great but it wasn't right. Maybe because he was drunk and she was sober but he didn't want them to be apart like this. He pulled her gently up towards him. "Come here."

They kissed again. It was better, her mouth and his. But in a minute she was off again, and this time he let her go.

He stretched out on his back. He felt he was on fire below the waist. But he couldn't connect with it. Images of his father were there. It was as if he should be guilty about what was happening, as if there should be no pleasure with his father dead. He wondered if she was enjoying herself, if she thought he was. Well, he was but it was remote, like watching a sexy scene at the pictures. He had never felt such a strangeness from her before. And yet he loved her more intensely than ever. What was going on? He lay there with her mouth on his prick, trying to connect.

There was a good turn-out at the funeral. His parents had stayed in the same town for more than thirty years—in fact Robert had been born not long after they settled there—so his father was well-known and well-liked. He was a joiner to trade, but in later years, when the money was more plentiful, he'd concentrated on his real love and art as a cabinetmaker. The house was full of fine pieces of furniture, all dove-tailed joints and inlays and carved feet, and he'd made a lot of stuff to order as well. The Minister paid special tribute to his skills. A craftsman, he said, one who loved detail and sought perfection in all he did. A good father and loving husband. An honest man. A kind man. A true friend to Scotland. In such phrases the man in the pulpit touched on the aspects of his father's life. Robert felt as though he were hearing these things for the first time. It was like reading his own obituary—or the obituary of the man he would like to be.

And then there was the burial itself, the lowering of his father into the ground. He was at the head of the grave, his mother and his sisters on either side of him. It was a beautiful day—he could tell people kept biting their tongues to stop themselves from saying how lucky they were with the weather. And yet they were lucky. A miserable, gloomy occasion it would have been in winter.

The sunshine put him in mind of his childhood here in this town. Holding the cord reminded him of holding the string of a kite. One year, when he was about ten or eleven, there was a craze for kites. All summer long the hill behind the town wore kites in the sky like a garland of bright flowers. There might be ten or fifteen of them up there at any time, traditional diamond-shaped kites, box kites, kites in the shape of birds and planes, and even one like a skull-and-crossbones. It looked so exciting from the bottom of the hill, it looked like the best thing in the world to be doing. So of course he had to have one.

But funnily enough once he got up there, with his red kite with its long tail, once he'd unwound the string to its full extent and was gripping the little tube at the end, everything lost its interest. You could make the kite dip and leap only so often. Then you withdrew from the other kite-fliers each bidding to outdo the tricks of the rest. And a new feeling came. You wanted to let the kite go. You didn't really but then you did. Let the kite fly off like a real thing, like a live thing, that's what you wanted.

146

He became aware again that he was standing over the grave. The coffin was being lowered and the others had released their cords onto the lid. The gravediggers had paused in letting down the straps and it was a moment before he understood that they were waiting for him. He heard a voice and felt the touch of a hand on his arm. "You have to let go now," said the voice. He didn't do it though, not deliberately, but still he felt the cord slip away through his fingers. Something fell from his face and landed on the wood. He found that he was crying.

He turned from the grave for a moment and wiped his eyes. It was daft, but he didn't want his father to see his tears. I don't want to be here any more, was what he was thinking. Then he waited, head bowed, while the Minister completed the words about the resurrection and the life.

There were sandwiches and tea and the harder stuff back at the house, for the family and close friends. Robert had heard his mother going among the folk at the service, picking them out: "You'll come back afterwards, won't you?" She was being very brave, very restrained. He wished he could be closer to her, but it was his dad he wanted.

The Minister was there, of course. It was some years since Robert had last seen him, let alone spoken to him.

"Would you say my father was religious?" he asked him.

The Minister had the grace to ponder this before nodding.

"Yes," he said. "But he baulked a little at the organisation. Like many of us these days." There was a smile playing about his lips, as if he were testing a heretical view. "He liked the product but not the firm that marketed it."

"That's because he believed in humanity," said Robert. "The Kirk sees humanity as an expression of God, of religion. He saw religion as an expression of humanity."

"I think you're being a wee bit unfair on the Kirk," said the Minister.

"Maybe," said Robert. "But that's the essence of it, isn't it? That struggle, I mean. Are we God's or is God ours? I don't go to church but I'm still religious. You can't change that. It's in

147

you, it's a state of mind."

The Minister said that that was good, in his opinion. He excused himself and moved on. Robert looked around for Kate. She was with one of his sisters across the room. She was wearing a neat little dark suit. She looked wonderful.

Robert's sister was admiring the little dark suit. Kate made the necessary smalltalk without much sense of being there, in that house after the funeral. She was thinking about what she and Robert would do next. She'd like them to go away, the two of them, just for a few days. It would do him good—to be somewhere else.

And she thought of that curious limbo they were in, that place between what they had and what they sought. They were whole people but they were less than whole because of how their country was. Yet she felt a confidence in herself, that she had reached an understanding of the situation. This was only a temporary lull. It might last a long time but it was only temporary. What she recognised in the hopelessness of the politics was her own hope, her complete inability to give up. That's the thing we have, she thought, the unbeatable hand that we may never play but which we always hold, the thing that they just don't understand. All we are doing is waiting.

He saw her across the room from him, and she seemed both very close and far away. Then he found himself thinking about the big things again: the earth spinning, and the pull of the moon on the tides, like the endless shuttle of a loom, the tide endlessly covering and laying bare all the world's beaches, and some-where in the west a long white empty beach, where the labours of the sea went unwitnessed by humans for generations. He thought about that empty beach, and where it might be, and he wanted to be there, to be away from all this, on a beach on the far side of an empty island, with nothing to look to but the moon-dragged sea. An island, and himself alone on it. And Kate would be there, but later. In such a place he would become small, insignificant, completely aware of the scale of things. He would step barefoot onto that pure white beach and leave his fleeting trail behind him as he walked down to the pure blue, ice-blue water, and he would watch the horizon rising to meet the sun and feel himself being tipped with the motion, there on the edge of the world. But then, at the moment of believing himself to be utterly alone, out beyond the line where the waves begin their roll, a seal's head would appear, bobbing, watching, as if to say, I am here, I am with you, I am beyond you, and the only answer that could form in his head would be the only one that matters: I love you, I love you, I love you.

Pretending to Sleep

I could stay here all day like this, pretending to sleep, and no one would know. No one would know how awake I really am.

Sometimes I even fool myself into thinking I'm asleep, and sometimes perhaps I do nod off for a minute or two, and sometimes—perhaps—I'm fooled by the dreams I have into thinking they're reality. I could tell a few dreams that I've had. But I don't think I'm going to. I'm just going to lie here, pretending to sleep.

Nobody tries to disturb you if they think you're sleeping. They can hardly believe that someone would stretch out in the middle of all their wakefulness and fall asleep, and it overawes them. They don't want to be the one to wake you, because they don't know what you're like. You might be cuddly or you might be crazy. You might roll over or you might bite. You're a sleeping dog—better to let you lie.

It's not just that they're afraid. They're envious too. If only they could stretch out in the sun or the rain, and not have to keep going, stay alert, be part of it. You're not part of it if you're sleeping, that's for sure. You can be right in the middle of things—in a street or a park—and you're separate, outside. You're something else.

Even the police leave you alone. There was a time when they would shake you awake and move you on, and if you slumped over ten yards further on they would lift you. Then you'd to sleep in the cells. There was no point in pretending there—you either slept or you didn't, and more often you didn't. You didn't care one way or the other but then again there wasn't anybody there to fool. Nobody could see you, except the guy who came every once in a while to check you weren't dead, and the only reason he came was because it would look bad if you died in his charge. Whether you lived or died was of no concern to him, so

150

long as you didn't die on his shift. But it's a long time since I've been lifted. These days the police are more enlightened. They don't see the harm in a wee sleep. Besides, they've plenty to keep them occupied. A sleeper is way down their list of priorities.

Funny how in the cells they come to check you're not dead. Out here, out in the open, nobody checks. Maybe as they pass they see your chest rise and fall—I don't know. But they never stop and touch you, stand over you, ask if you're all right. This is the fear again, the fear and the envy. They don't disturb you because you disturb them. Just by lying there, pretending to sleep, you get under their skin, like an itch, you get deep into them.

Sunny days are best but rain can be all right too. With enough layers on, it can take all day to soak through. And the effect on the people passing by is greater, it totally upsets them. A man lying asleep in the pouring rain is like a corpse at a table in a café. He shouldn't be there. He should have been tidied away. But he is there, and he can't be ignored.

Some people think they do ignore you, but they don't. You go into them just the same, but more subtly. You lodge yourself like a parasite in their brain, and they don't know why they're getting these terrible headaches. Long after they've forgotten you you're uncurling yourself in there, eating away at their consciousness, bugging them, you're something gnawing at the back of their mind. They don't remember the figure prone in the park, the drizzle, the slight rise and fall of the chest, but the memory's there just the same.

If I dream, the dream is that I'll never wake up. That's why I know the dreams are not real, because I'm not asleep at all. I'm wide awake, pretending. I do it for myself. And I'll say this, I do it for everyone else too. I do it for all the ones who can't sleep, who can't stop, who can't lie down in the street. I pretend on their behalf.

This is the thing. I pretend for them. They look at me and think I'm asleep, but I'm completely aware of myself, of what's going on. I know who's awake and who's not. I may fool them, but they don't fool me.

151

There's more of us this year than ever before. You'll have noticed. Every month there's more of us, sleeping out in the open, in broad daylight. I'm not talking about homelessness, that's another story, I'm talking about people who've had enough, who are prepared just to lie down and be counted, or not be counted, to fall asleep and make the crowds step round us.

Only we're not asleep. I've told you that. We're just pretending. You're getting so used to us that you keep forgetting that important point.

One day you're in for the fright of your fucking life.